ARLENE McFARLANE

Murder, Curlers & Kilts

A Valentine Beaumont
Mini Mystery

ISBN-13: 978-0-9953076-9-8

Published by ParadiseDeer Publishing
Canada

Cover Art by Sue Traynor
Formatting by Author E.M.S.

Praise for
Murder, Curlers & Kilts

"Zany characters, lots of laughs, and a murder mystery that will keep you turning pages!"

–*New York Times* Bestselling Author, Christie Craig

"A sexy, laugh-out-loud puzzler! I can't wait to visit Rueland again!"

–*USA Today* Bestselling Author, Leslie Langtry

"Mayhem, murder, and mascara—it's all in a day's work for Valentine Beaumont, the world's most entertaining crime-solving stylist. Set at an international festival, with a killer cast of quirky characters, including sexy investigator Romero, *Murder, Curlers & Kilts* will entertain fans of both mystery and romance novels."

–Diane Kelly, award-winning author of the House Flipper, Paw Enforcement, and Death & Taxes series

"A fun and flirty, killer good time!"

–*New York Times* Bestselling Author, Addison Moore

"Laughs and mystery abound in this fantastic book. Fans of Janet Evanovich will love this twist on crime in a small town!"

–*New York Times* Bestselling Author, Shirley Jump

Acknowledgments

Warmest thanks to Forensics Federal Agent Geoff Symon and Sergeant Patrick O'Donnell for graciously answering my many questions. Any inaccuracies in these pages were intended for a more entertaining read.

Deepest appreciation also to award-winning, *New York Times*, and *USA Today* Bestselling Authors Addison Moore, Christie Craig, Shirley Jump, Diane Kelly, and Leslie Langtry for your tremendous endorsements. As gifted and respected authors, you've been a huge inspiration to me.

Karen Dale Harris, Noël Kristan Higgins, Amy Atwell, and Sue Traynor: I cherish you all and couldn't ask for a more efficient or hard-working squad.

My dearest, faithful followers (insert millions of glittery hearts): If you're reading this book, you've likely devoured the series. I'm truly grateful for your loyalty, your desire to laugh, and your love for Valentine. I can most certainly guarantee she loves you right back!

My little family: As always, you've championed me in countless ways and blessed me with your individual strengths. You fill my heart daily with joy. xoxo

My gratitude begins and ends with God, our Creator. I continue to put my faith in You.

To my father:

You always liked a good laugh...truly one of life's gifts.

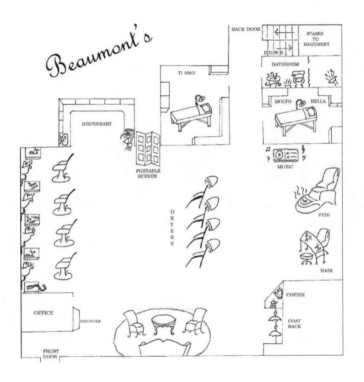

Chapter 1

My name is Valentine Beaumont. I'm the sole proprietor of Beaumont's, a fair to middling beauty salon in the heart of Rueland, Massachusetts. I knew my day was off to a bad start when Phyllis, one of my employees, traipsed her first client this morning into Ti Amo, one of the treatment rooms, for an underarm wax, and the customer stomped out of the salon thirty minutes later with chunks of the depilatory strung from her ears.

Phyllis lacks genius when it comes to beautifying others. But I keep her on because a) she's a remote family member, and b) the elderly patrons believe she's a hard worker despite their botched colors and ruined cuts. If they were happy, who was I to rock the boat? Plus, if I let Phyllis go, like I had once done a while back, there'd be hell to pay from my mother's aunts—women who made Disney's sea witch Ursula seem sweeter than Cinderella's fairy godmother.

We locked up at two, our usual closing time on Saturday, and I joined a thousand people in Rueland Town Park for the annual May multicultural festival. Kids were stuffing their faces with cotton candy, the Ferris wheel was in full swing, and a blend of dialects and music from bagpipes to steel drums echoed in the air. Every country under the sun was represented, and my heart warmed with pride that my hometown hosted such a diverse event.

I promised my parents I'd help dish out shish kebab, tabbouleh, and samples of hummus in the Armenian booth. But at the moment, I sank my sparkly heels in the lush grass, mouth gaping at Phyllis twelve feet away, pacing behind a yard-sale table.

Phyllis was squashed into an unevenly pleated plaid kilt—clearly one of her sewing creations—with a matching tam perched on her head. She was waving what looked like an old Sony Walkman in an Asian man's face.

As much as I wanted to flee, I couldn't tear myself away from witnessing what would happen next.

"You take one dollar?" The man nodded his head in earnest at Phyllis despite her resembling a Rueland-Memorial-psych-ward escapee.

"One dollar!" Phyllis pushed back her tam, her mahogany curls frizzed underneath. "What do you think this is? A charity? Ten dollars, firm."

"But this is from 1980. So long ago."

"What's the year got to do with it? Sony's a good name. Everyone knows that." She shoved up her sleeves, a sure sign she was readying for battle.

A tremor of anxiety inched its way up my spine. Phyllis was losing her patience, and the outcome wasn't going to be pretty.

The tentative buyer wore a camera around his neck, and from where I was standing at the far side of the table, a look of confusion on his face. Barbeque smells rose through the park. Ethnic songs played in the background. But he was deaf to everything except the Walkman. He studied it good and hard, pressing buttons, shaking the gadget by his ear. He checked that batteries were in place, then pushed the eject button. He pulled out the cassette, examined it, snapped it back inside, and pressed the buttons again. Nothing.

"Look"—Phyllis slung her hands on her hips—"I haven't got all day. Do you want the thing or not?"

The man frowned at Phyllis in her bagpipe outfit, then turned sideways and looked at me for help.

I was a crappy whistler, but I puckered up and whistled a ditty, pretending to take interest in a German vendor churning out beer nuts a few stalls over.

The poor guy swiveled back to Phyllis and held up the Walkman. "But it doesn't work."

Phyllis narrowed her eyes, suspicion etched across her face. "I know your kind of shopper. You'll get that Walkman home, take it apart, make a few adjustments, and in no time, it'll be good as new, playing show tunes from *The Mikado*. In fact, it'll be worth *twice* the price."

The guy's mouth dropped open, and his eyes rolled high into his head. Probably never met anyone like Phyllis before.

Wagering it'd only go downhill from here, I spun around to leave and bumped into Maximilian Martell, my second-in-command at Beaumont's. Also, my best male friend.

"You're going to miss the next event!" He towed me a foot away, his hazel eyes lit with excitement. Then he pulled up straight, catching sight of Phyllis in her plaid skirt and tam. "What's Mary, Queen of Scots doing?"

Max. Always the shallow approach.

"She's selling a broken Walkman to that gentleman."

He crossed his arms in front. "Should I tell the poor fellow I've got an ax and chopping block with her name on it?"

He also lived to rattle Phyllis. I backhanded him in the stomach. "Don't be mean. Not everyone has a perverse interest in historic beheadings like you."

"Maybe they should." He rubbed his gut. "Historical facts shaped the world we live in."

Oh brother.

He dragged his stare away from Phyllis and did a double take of me. "I thought there was something different on you today. You're wearing false eyelashes."

I batted my lashes playfully. "How can you tell?"

He was an inch from my nose. "For starters, your left lashes aren't glued down properly. Secondly, you should've trimmed them. It looks like you've got tarantulas on your eyelids."

I sliced him a dirty look. Max was so skilled at his job he could make an old bag lady with rotten teeth and bad hair look like a fashion model. And he could do it blindfolded. Still, I didn't need his analysis. To tell the truth, the lashes did seem excessive, their weight and thickness almost obstructing my view. I pressed down the lash on the outer corner of my left eyelid, giving him a sticky blink.

"Why are you even wearing false eyelashes?" he wanted to know. "You've got the longest, thickest lashes I've ever seen. With those amber eyes of yours, you don't need extra glitz."

"One of the salesmen left me a pair to try," I said, ignoring his flattery, "so I thought, why not?"

"I just told you why not." He let his words sink in, then gazed back at Phyllis. "On the topic of needing extra glitz, what's going on with our lassie's hair today? Bozo the Clown never had so much frizz."

I shrugged. "She blamed this morning's dew."

He thought about this, utter disbelief on his face. "A talented stylist would've used any number of hair products to tame the frizz. Of course, no one could ever accuse Phyllis of being a talented stylist."

I leaned my arm against Max's shoulder, slid off one of my heels, and rubbed the ball of my foot. It'd been an especially busy workday—the dewy morning bringing in a stream of clients—and the less standing around I did in four-inch spikes, the better.

Max knit his eyebrows together while holding me up. "How was she allowed to set up a yard-sale table at a multicultural fair, anyway? Last time I checked, there were no cultural roots in worthless items."

I gave my other foot the same treatment. "Good question. Ask Phyllis."

He did a not-on-your-life head shake, then jumped at the Asian man's yelp.

"Lady!" the guy cried at Phyllis. "You're crazy!" He dropped the Walkman on her table with a loud clank and stalked away.

"And you have dandruff!" Phyllis shouted to his back.

"Another happy customer," Max muttered.

A huge, noisy thump sounded at the far side of the park near a large pond, catching our attention. Hundreds of cheers followed. "Come *on*." Max yanked my arm. "You're going to miss it."

"Miss what?" Phyllis trooped over and bobbed her head past us at the crowd surrounded by dozens of international flags.

"The caber toss," Max said. "Jock's about to throw the pole. I can't wait to see how he stacks up against the Scots."

Speaking of stacking up. Jock de Marco, at six three— or four, is my third employee, an Argentinean with shiny, hard muscles who made Mr. Universe look like an undersized adolescent.

Max eased his grip on me and glared up and down at Phyllis. "I may be sorry for asking, but what are you doing dressed up like a Highland dancer? You're not Scottish. And your pleats, by the way, are lopsided."

Phyllis browsed down at her kilt, then back up at Max in his up-to-the-minute fitted shirt and tailored pants. "So I veered from the pattern. It's the best I could do on short notice."

Max rolled his eyes. "You call a fair held every year on the same weekend in May *short notice*?"

"At least I *dressed* for the occasion. And there's got to be some Scottish in me." She adjusted her tam that kept falling over her forehead. "I have red hair, don't I?"

"That's from a bottle, you idiot."

"I'm Scottish, I tell you." She tugged down her skirt. "And I'm as strong as an ox. If those blokes can fling a tree trunk, so can I." She marched toward the field, fist in the air. Braveheart leading the troops into battle.

Max shrugged, his eyebrows hiked up to his streaked blond hairline. "I always said you could plow a field with Phyllis. But this I gotta see."

We trailed behind Phyllis past an Australian boomerang toss, a group of bagpipers wailing out a melody, a game of cricket, and a sumo wrestling match.

"Hey, Phyll." Max tapped her shoulder. "Wouldn't you rather grab a loincloth? Sumo wrestling seems more your style."

Phyllis shooed his hand away and whirled around. "I wouldn't lower my standards to wrestle with the likes of those two blubbery animals. If you ask me, they should get out of the ring and into Weight Watchers."

"What's good for the goose..." Max sang. He swung his saucy gaze to me, scrutinized my death glare, then choked back the rest of the saying.

"Look," I said, "I promised my mother I'd be at their booth by three." I peered down at my mauve dress. "Bad enough I didn't have time after my last walk-in to suit up in my ethnic gear, but she's not going to be thrilled I'm late. So if you want me to witness Jock tossing a piece of wood, let's get to it. Time's a-ticking."

I aimed for the field when we heard, "You-hoo! Ducky!"

Now what?

I turned around with the others, ready to greet the familiar voice that belonged to either Betty or Birdie Cutler, identical-sounding English twin sisters and clients. Instead, I bumped into a mascot resembling a globe, with blue tights, big white gloves, and huge padded feet. I apologized to the mascot as it went on its way and focused my attention on the twins skipping toward us.

The Cutlers were mid-fifties and among the wealthiest of my clients. They were in matching spring dresses, aprons around their waists, and they had a plump man in tow. The guy was short with thinning fair hair and wore a red T-shirt that kept rising above his belly. There was something cartoonish about him. I couldn't decide if he was more Winnie the Pooh or Porky Pig. I guessed him to be about thirty-five, but his dimply smile made him seem years younger.

"This is Emery," Birdie said after the hellos, her British accent refined. "Our own little godsend. Took a break from work and helped us set up our stall this year since Hedley's down with a cold."

Hedley was the Cutlers' butler and jack of all trades.

Emery hiccupped a laugh. "Gosh, ladies, happy to do it."

Betty took me aside and whispered in my ear. "Poor Emery's menial desk job is so dreary, but we do what we can to encourage him."

The Cutlers were famous for taking less-fortunates under their wings, giving them praise and support when needed. They'd done this for one of my deliverymen who'd been wrongfully accused of murder. "Giving back to the community," they liked to say.

"We've got bangers and mash on the grill at our booth," Birdie went on, "and *authentic* English-style fish and chips." To that, they both gave a proud nod. "Come over and try some."

The term *bangers* took me back to my reunion with escaped convict Ziggy Stoaks and the last case I'd solved. Another part of Valentine Beaumont. Full-time beautician. Part-time sleuth. Famous for apprehending a nutbar killer by wrapping a perm rod around his bangers. Ziggy's term, not mine.

To be honest, I didn't advertise that I caught crooks by wielding my beauty tools. There were enough reminders from well-intentioned folks every time they spotted me with my black beauty bag. Thing was, my tools doubled nicely as weapons, especially when faced with life-and-death situations. Sure, it took imagination and ingenuity. But that was me. The resourceful child.

Because of my close call with Ziggy, the thought of eating sausage and creamed potatoes was far from appealing. "Thanks," I said, "but we're on our way to see Jock throw the caber."

At the mention of Lord de Marco, the sisters batted *their* firmly-glued-on lashes and swallowed simultaneously. Hardly able to contain themselves, they quivered up and down, their A-cupped breasts standing at attention.

I'd seen this reaction on most women who'd met Jock. And why wouldn't they quiver? Jock was God's gift to humanity. Strong. Powerful. Handsome. Hercules on earth. He was also honorable and one hell of a stylist. No wonder everyone admired him. *I* admired him. Maybe too much for an employer-employee relationship. Something I continually fought to keep in check.

"Bugger!" Betty exclaimed. "Wouldn't that be smashing to see, but we need to get back to our booth."

Emery hiked up his pants that were falling below his waist, then gestured his pudgy arm toward the action. "Gosh, if you want to see your friend toss the caber, I can watch the booth for a while."

Betty gave me a nudge. "Emery tries," she whispered, "but he's a bit on the clumsy side. I'm afraid he'd burn down the stall." She turned to Emery and brightened. "No need, pet. We'll come along." She slid her arm through his and looked back over her shoulder at me. "Next hair appointment, tell us what we missed."

I did a thumbs up, then swung around to Max and Phyllis, half of the dynamic duo nowhere in sight. "What happened to Phyllis?"

Max pointed to the caber-toss area where shouts and merriment filled the air. "She went to get her place." He grinned. "You ready for your laugh of the day?"

I blinked, impressed with the hundreds of spectators. The caber toss was obviously the most popular event in the park. "Ready as I'll ever be."

We traipsed over to the field where half a dozen strapping men in kilts lined up, waiting to hurl the caber. Then there was Phyllis, the runt of the litter, socking an imaginary punching bag. I guess it hadn't sunk in that this was tossing, not boxing.

All went silent as a large, bearded, redheaded man strode up to the plate. He gave a full body shake, loosening up, and did a few knee bends. Then he winched up the caber and sent it flying ten feet off to the side. There were groans, *oh no's*, and other glum remarks. I clapped and gave a *woo-hoo*, amazed someone could lift a sixteen-foot pole and throw it that far.

"Shh." Max tugged my hands down. "He didn't flip the caber forward at twelve o'clock like he was supposed to." He stretched his neck past the spectators in front of us, a smile inching up his face. "He does do a kilt justice though." He craned his neck further. "Speaking of doing a kilt justice, look who's up next."

I skimmed past the cluster and spotted Jock, heads above his competition, in a purple plaid kilt undoubtedly tailored for him, his long, chestnut brown hair flowing past his collar. He loosened the buttons on his white shirt, rolled back his shoulders in a fluid, sensual motion, then walked over to his caber.

Max leaned in. "You think it's true what they say about men in kilts?"

A lady in front of us turned around, fanning her face. "I'm willing to find out."

Max chuckled at that. Meanwhile, I reluctantly let my gaze follow the smooth lines of Jock's fitted shirt down to his kilt that defined his muscular thighs. A shot of heat soared through me, and I strangled back a cough. I knew what the lady meant. I'd probably have erotic dreams for weeks, wondering what was beneath Jock's kilt. *Baloney. You already know what's beneath, thanks to last fall's cruise.*

I refrained from also fanning my face, not wanting to cause a draft on my lashes. At least that was what I told myself. Truth was, I wasn't about to give Max ammunition when it came to Jock. I had a hard enough time keeping the lines from blurring.

A low hush deepened in the crowd. Music faded, the soft breeze waned, and I could've sworn splashing ducks held their wings. The anticipation in the air was so tense, time stood still while everyone waited for Jock to heave the caber.

He stood over the pole, hands on hips, Paul Bunyan in the flesh. A few deep breaths later, he surveyed the crowd, his caramel-flecked, brown-eyed gaze pinning mine. He gave a captivating wink, and at once the same lady in front of us, along with several others, twirled around to see who it was directed at.

My cheeks burned, and I hastily stared at the grass, finding nothing more fascinating than patches of dirt and fresh dandelions sprouting up.

The emcee introduced Jock over the microphone, gushing that his caber was twenty-five feet long and two hundred pounds. If Jock merely lifted the caber off the ground, it'd be an unparalleled success.

The mob roared. They knew they were in for a treat.

Muscles rippled through Jock's shirt as he put his all into hoisting the pole. He walked a few paces to gain momentum, then with the ease of carrying a branch, he flipped it straight forward at twelve o'clock, not once, but two times.

"A perfect execution!" the emcee cried. "And a double topple!"

The fans went ballistic. Women cheered and threw confetti popcorn. Men clapped each other on the back. Max gave one of his ear-piercing whistles. Me, I was waiting for something spectacular to happen.

"Did you *see* that?" Max caught his breath like he was the one who'd accomplished the feat.

I sighed. "Yes. Amazing."

His face soured. "You don't look amazed."

Honestly, it was grating how easily Jock could win over a crowd. If it wasn't bucking a caber, it was fixing airplane engines or speaking a multitude of languages. Well, not everyone had Jock's talents or superhuman strength. Some of us were plain mortals. Not something I wished to bemoan with Max. He worshipped the ground Jock walked on.

I forced up the corners of my lips. "Better?"

Max gave me a skeptical frown. "Now you look like the village idiot."

Once the throng settled down from viewing "The Jock de Marco Show," Phyllis tramped up to the plate. The announcer seemed confused as to who she was and why she was there, but Phyllis made short work of him. She grabbed the microphone and gave a three-minute rendition of her life.

"And for any of you press out there," she said in closing, "that's Murdoch with an *H*."

"And Dimwit with a *D*," Max murmured.

She slapped the mic back in the emcee's hand, waltzed over to her spot, inhaled like the big bad wolf, and lugged the pole into her interlocked hands.

She did pretty well, lurching forward and back a few times, her legs not buckling from the strain. Then there was sudden panic in her face as if she realized she didn't know what to do next. Sweat poured down her cheeks, her staggering became uncontrolled, and her eyes bled fear. I'd seen this look before and made a move to run over and help, but Max hauled me back, one of us recognizing I was powerless to do anything.

"Watch out, Phyllis!" Max flapped his arms at her in alarm. "You're heading for the pond!"

Phyllis stumbled around in circles. The herd of gawkers—laying bets on the outcome—swayed to and fro with her steps. Not able to manage any longer, she rocked back toward the spectators, then forward toward the water, crashing the caber into the pond with a gut-wrenching howl.

A huge tidal wave splashed thirty feet in every direction, soaking half the crowd. A canoe that had been docked at the water's edge sprang up like a fountain, unleashing something from underneath.

"Incoming!" someone shouted, sending everyone for cover.

Max tried to pull me out of the way from the missile aiming for us, but my spikes had sunk into the earth, leaving me immobile.

Suddenly, there was a *whump* on the ground next to me, the force lifting my heels out of the soil. But it wasn't a missile at all. It was a bloated, algae-covered body of a man in a kilt.

Chapter 2

Phyllis slumped to the ground by the shore, and I screamed for the stars. Not unusual since I usually shrieked or hurled things when shocked. Everyone closed in to ogle the greenish, swollen corpse that had seaweed tangled in its neat brown beard and clipped hair.

A putrid odor rose from the victim that overpowered the food smells in the park. One woman fainted, and several others lost their lunch. Most backed away, trying to compose themselves before they, too, went down.

I caught my breath and willed myself to keep *my* lunch from coming up. With one hand on my stomach, I felt behind me for Max.

"Over here, lovey."

I swiveled around and saw Max ten feet away, pinching his nose.

"What are you doing?" I almost didn't recognize my hoarse voice.

"Deep breathing, *away* from that Creature from the Black Lagoon."

I teetered over to him, controlling myself. "We've got to phone the police. No one's doing anything except looking for a clean spot to vomit."

"Why bother calling?" Max coughed, hand over his mouth. "Romero's over there."

"Romero?" My voice softened, my gaze following Max's gesture toward the huge Ferris wheel and the multitude of international booths scattered below.

"Yes. You know. Michael, the detective? Mr. Long Arm of the Law? Six-foot-tall wall of sexy cop? Dangerously handsome. Sapphire eyes that I swear are lined with kohl, and incidentally, which I would kill for." He was so wound up over Romero, he'd forgotten about the rotting smell and puffy corpse. "How do you resist him?"

A dozen questions ran through my mind. Resist Romero? Huh. Last time I'd seen him, we were in a hot and heavy tussle that had to do with my refusal to take a battery of self-defense courses. It started with a minor disagreement and Romero using official cop jargon to intimidate me. Then it progressed to a playful scuffle with me poking him in the chest countless times, brandishing my extensive use of sarcasm and smartass humor. It ended with Romero throwing me down on the floor, showing me unequivocally how easy it'd be for an attacker to pin me down, with or without my bag of tools to protect me.

Though I should've been furious with Romero for overpowering me, the skirmish turned sensual. His strength and raw hunger turned me on, blowing through my oath to take things slow. That was Martin Luther King Jr. Day, a federal holiday like any other, and we were doing our part to celebrate.

We were tearing at each other's clothes when Romero got a call that a riot had broken out in Boston. The riot was tied to a cybercrime double homicide he'd been working. The case had roots in Louisiana, and up until that point, he'd managed to stave off traveling there, carrying out his end of the case from Massachusetts. But the party was over. I was still catching my breath when he gave me his house key and told me to stay as long as I wished. Then he was gone. Off to Baton Rouge.

My heart throbbed and my throat ached, the harsh reality hitting me. We'd gone three-and-a-half months without seeing each other. Had the physical distance changed things between us? Had the time apart lessened his desire for me? We'd been in touch, but why hadn't he phoned when he'd returned? I'd lamented his absence to Max more than once, and his response was always, "He'll be back."

The frown I was wearing said sure he'd be back, but where were we at?

Noticing my disheartened look, Max pounded a fist in his palm like he knew what was tormenting me. "If that S-O-B is giving you the heave-ho, he's going to answer to me. That ratfink. That scoundrel."

"A minute ago, you were calling him sexy and dangerously handsome."

He stopped pounding and aligned himself. "I was, wasn't I? Sorry, sister. You're on your own."

What did I ever do to deserve Max? "Gee, thanks."

I peered back at the mob and the dead body, then took a shaky breath and headed toward the exhibition area.

"I'd be careful if I were you," Max cried out from behind my back. "He's not going to be happy when you tell him what you stumbled on…again."

I twisted around with little finesse, thanks to the soil sucking at my heels. "I didn't unearth this body. Phyllis did."

While that was true, I couldn't stop trembling or eliminate the goose bumps covering my flesh in anticipation of running into Romero. One thing was certain. I'd stick to the matter at hand. There was a dead man in the park. Didn't mean it was murder. Didn't mean it wasn't. And my being here was totally coincidental.

I reached down, swiped away the chunks of dirt wedged to my heel, and felt something loosen from the muck in my hand. I rubbed off the item and revealed an oval stone glowing from turquoise to purple. I held it up under my nose, looking closer as I removed the last bits of debris. It wasn't merely a stone. It was a ring. A mood ring.

I retraced my steps. How'd it lodge in my heel? Did someone drop it? I looked down at the ground, then up at Max who was on his way over to Phyllis resting by the water's edge. I guess we all needed a few minutes to take stock of what had just happened.

I shook off the horrible vision and slid the ring over my thumb since it was too large to fit on any other finger. If I didn't find who owned it, it'd be interesting to see what the ring told me about my moods…if it revealed anything.

I carried on in search of Romero. I passed the Hungarian and Spanish tents and rushed by the Swedish booth where meatballs were simmering in a sweet-smelling sauce. I took a long slow breath and forced down a swallow. Of all times to lose my appetite.

Rounding the corner to the next row of booths, another smell wafted my way. Oregano-rich pizza sauce. I took another lungful of air to quell the nausea in my stomach and combed the area for the source of the aroma.

Through the swarm of festivalgoers, I looked to my right and spotted Romero behind a grill, under a canopy, flipping panzerottis. At first glance, I noted his hair had grown another inch, his jaw was unshaved, and he was sporting a gorgeous tan, darkening his Mediterranean skin. His denim shirt tugged across his broad shoulders, his sleeves rolled up past his muscled forearms while he worked the spatula in his hand.

I wiped my brow with the back of my wrist, and before my eyes, the mood ring on my thumb changed from turquoise and purple to yellow. I examined the gleaming stone. Boy, that was quick. Must be telling me I was seriously Romero-deprived.

Nonsense. I'd ask Twix Bonelli, my best friend since ballet class, what she thought. She'd had a mood ring in high school and revered its many shades and meanings.

It took a few moments gawking at Romero to get my act together. The closer I looked, the more visible were the tension lines around his mouth. Exhaustion drew the corners of his eyes down. This was a man who'd seen the violent side of death, the greed and hatred that reared their ugly heads in a multitude of ways and often ended in tragedy. His was a job that demanded strength of character, patience, tolerance. A job many wouldn't want.

Two attractive women lingered by the stall, openly flirting with Romero. At one time, he would've flirted back, giving them his full attention. But he kept busy at the grill, barely noticing them. Either his mind was on the load I sensed he carried, or he was done with those games.

Seeing him engrossed in his work and warding off the sexual advances brought on a carnal rush followed by nervous fluttering. I lost all thought, including where I was and how queasy I felt.

I looked from Romero to the green-white-and-red striped flag above the canopy beside a banner that said *ITALY*. Right. Multicultural fair. Cadaver in the park. Get help.

The two women finally took off, dejected, and a rush of adoration struck my heart at Romero's actions. But this girl wasn't about to let tender emotions rule her head. Romero hadn't told me he was home, and as far as I was concerned, he was—to borrow from Max—a rat fink. I put my chin up, inhaled brusquely to gain my wits, and strutted over to the booth like, *this is my town, baby.*

Romero ducked to get something under the counter, then surfaced and caught my eye. I broke into a coughing fit, the smoke from his grill snagging in my throat. Sputtering to right myself, I succeeded in gagging and choking more. I gasped for air and bent over to let it out.

"Don't stand there, ye eejit," came a female voice from behind the counter. "Go help the lass. Here, give her some fizzy juice."

Taking another gulp of air, I straightened in time to see Romero stroll toward me, a can of Sprite in his toned hand, his Iron Man watch loosely strapped to his wrist, an amused look in his eyes. "Here. Drink this."

Too worked up to comment on the look or the white apron tied around his lean waist, I swiped the soda from him and downed the contents. Not exactly the way I'd planned our reunion.

Dismissing Romero's assessing gaze, I centered on the tiny woman with short gray hair who'd appeared and spoken. *Perfect.* Romero's mother, Aileen. We'd met months ago at Romero's sister's wedding.

Though Aileen had moved from Scotland to Italy when she married Romero's father, she'd never lost her Scottish accent, even after coming to the States. I prayed she hadn't remembered me. "Thank you." I nodded first to her, then to Romero.

He angled his head down to meet my gaze, his piercing blue eyes darkening, his deep voice turned low. "You okay?"

Under other circumstances, I would've melted from his sexy, rugged tone and subtly alluring Arctic Spruce scent that was currently teasing my senses. Instead, I sniffed primly. "Good as new."

He gave me one of his lingering stares, the kind that said he had me all figured out, the kind that made me feel like he was stripping me bare without even touching me. If that wasn't enough, his eyes were fixed on my lashes, the familiar twitch at the corner of his mouth telling me he was holding back a grin.

Damn things. Big deal. Didn't take a PhD or a know-it-all police detective to deduce I was dabbling in luxury cosmetics.

I nonchalantly pressed down the outer edge of my lashes and plunged ahead. I wasn't going to broach the subject of Romero's absence or, more importantly, his return. I was here for a reason.

Gravely, I recalled the bloated, discolored body lying in the field. "There's been an accident. Of sorts," I added, fidgeting with the soda can to hide the shudder fighting to resurface.

He took the Sprite from my hands and set it on the counter. Then he planted his fists on his hips, as if he knew what he was about to learn wouldn't make him happy. "What kind of an accident?"

I stuffed down the dread growing in my bones. "The kind involving a dead body." I lowered my head, hoping my lashes would hide my face.

He took his finger and lifted my chin, then crossed his arms in front. "Why is that the kind you're always involved in?"

I shrugged, and before I had a chance to say anything, his mother scurried out beside us and pinched Romero's forearm. "Mind your manners. Can't ye see the bonnie lass is upset?"

Romero rubbed his arm, disregarding the jibe. "Not as upset as I'm going to be after I hear her news." He waited until my eyes settled on him, then tipped his head at me. "What is it this time? Somebody crash-dive from a hot air balloon? Get trampled on by a herd of elephants?" He swung his gaze to the far side of the park. "Or maybe one of those kilted lumberjacks drowned in the pond."

I pointed my finger in the air. "Bingo."

"What are ye talking aboot?" Aileen wiped her palms on her apron, then took my shaking hands and rubbed them in hers, her sharp blue gaze a soft replica of Romero's. "A drowning? Here? In the park?"

I nodded. "I'm not sure he was in line to toss lumber. But he *was* wearing a kilt."

It was her turn to plant her hands on her hips. "Ye heard the lass." She stared up at her son. "What are ye gonna do now?"

Romero put his arm around her shoulder and rested his chin on top of her head. "Go for a beer? Cybercrimes and scammers cheating old ladies out of their grocery money are putting a dent in my cheery disposition." He ruffled Aileen's hair. "And considering I flew in on the red-eye to help you out at the festival—despite being in the middle of five cases—I think I owe it to myself."

She swatted his arm away. "Don't be cheeky. Valentine's come to you for help. That all you're gonna say?"

Valentine? She remembered me?

He drew her closer and gave me a suggestive grin. "I'll have more to say later." His penetrating gaze flooded me with uneasy anticipation. Then he took a step back and called in the incident.

Brute. I remained firm, tightening my thighs all the same to keep them from quivering from the promise in his eyes.

"What did he look like, dear?" Aileen pulled me back to the conversation as if she were taking over the case. "Apart from wearing the kilt."

I closed my eyes for a second, drawing on what I could remember. "Late thirties, stylish beard, short haircut, a tad longer on top." Okay, those were the things I discerned first. I was a beautician, wasn't I?

"He was also well-built but not extremely tall. Maybe five-ten." I thought for a moment. "I couldn't be sure because of the filth covering him, but it looked like he had a bruise or welt on the side of his head."

Romero was back, listening intently. "Festival duty cops should be there shortly. Plus, we'll get a team down." He gave me a nod. "How close to the victim did you say you were?"

"Close enough to know what I saw."

"Hmm." Aileen shook her head, thinking this through. "Five-ten. Well-built. Stylish beard." She squinted over her shoulder. "With beards all the rage today, that could be half the men in the park."

I bit on a nail, asking myself if I'd missed anything, when the ring's glow caught my attention. I took off the ring and set it in my palm. "I also found this stuck to my heel."

Aileen tilted her head down, giving my sparkly shoes a curious stare. It took everything in me not to fidget. I knew I wasn't exactly the girl next door, and for some reason, I cared what she thought.

Her astute gaze moved its way up my fitted mauve dress, settled briefly at my cleavage, then rose to my glittery earrings and burgundy hair that fell halfway down my back in loose curls. Finally, the appraisal rested on the tarantulas on my eyelids, which I fought to bat innocently.

She didn't say a word. What's more, she bestowed me with an easy smile, the kind free of judgment. That, and the way she'd smoothed my hands earlier, told me we were already friends.

She edged in to take a better look at the stone that was merging colors. "I've seen this ring before." She gawked up at Romero. "Does it look familiar to you?"

Romero bent to study it, then gave a head shake. "Could belong to anyone."

Aileen wasn't deterred. "Where'd ye first notice it stuck to your shoe, dear?"

"Over by the—" Then it hit me.

I explained how I'd been standing in the field, watching Phyllis toss the caber into the pond. Water had sprayed everywhere from the impact, and the victim, who'd been trapped under a canoe, shot out of the water and landed next to me. The ring could've been on his finger. When he thundered to the ground, it must've freed itself and rolled in the dirt until it was next to my shoe.

Ick. I shook the ring away from me, and it dropped at our feet. "You don't suppose it could've belonged to the deceased, do you?"

Romero gave me a glare.

"It's just a casual interest." I summoned courage, trying not to get hoity-toity from his stare.

He squatted and picked up the ring with a pen from his shirt pocket. "I will say this. Depending on how long the victim was submerged in water, his fingers would've likely swollen. Then again, the ring could've been loose to begin with. If he hit the ground as hard as you're saying, it's possible the ring could've bounced off."

Aileen's eyes widened. "That's it! I knew I'd seen this ring before. Woody MacDunnell was wearing it last night when we were setting up for the weekend." She paused. "He looked so handsome in his kilt. They all did."

"All?" I asked.

"The Scots. They looked dapper in their kilts, standing out last night from everyone else wearing jeans. But back to the ring. Halfway through setup, we'd all taken a break for coffee and donuts from Friar Tuck's that the fair committee provided."

Friar Tuck's sat next to Beaumont's and resembled a mini castle straight out of Sherwood Forest. Drinks were served in pewter mugs, and staff wore tights like Robin Hood's Merry Men. It was a bit overkill, and employees weren't thrilled by their uniforms. But their donuts were supreme.

"When I got to the table, I reached for the same apple fritter as Woody." She gave me a nudge. "They're my favorite. And that's when I saw his ring, glowing a translucent green. Added to everything you've said, Woody fits the description perfectly."

A worried look crossed her face, and she crooked her neck from me to Romero. "Didn't think anything of it before, but I heard him arguing with Malton MacGregor last night around nine when we left the park."

"Who's Malton MacGregor?" I asked.

"An ignorant sod." Romero dumped the ring and pen in his shirt pocket, then checked a message on his phone. "He's had a few run-ins with the law. Guy wouldn't think twice about selling his sister for a cigarette." He tapped a response on his phone, then came back to the conversation again, motioning to Aileen. "My mother used to belong to a knitting club with his mother."

I let my gaze roam past the row of booths to where I saw the Scottish flag fluttering above a blue-and-white canopy. "And he's here, working a stand?"

"Looks like it." Romero scanned the area. "Probably trying to figure a way to con the organizers out of money."

I pursed my lips, contemplating this. "Do you think there could be a connection to Woody's death?" So I was asking too many questions for someone with a casual interest.

He overlooked my comment and put his hand on Aileen's shoulder, his sense of urgency building. "What was the argument about?"

Aileen shrugged. "Couldn't tell, but they were having quite a row."

Romero gave me the eye. In other words, *stay out of it*.

His mother pushed him toward the field. "Gaun yersel'. Do your job and don't mind Valentine. The lass is peely-wally. What she needs is color put back in her cheeks." She gave me the same wink Romero often gave—without the sexy connotation.

I lowered my thick lashes, feeling good about where I stood with Romero's mother, when I sensed his stare lingering on me. I peeked up at him, his silence telling me he knew just the thing to put color in my cheeks.

My heart gave a raucous thump, and I choked back another coughing fit that had nothing to do with the smoking grill.

Confident I got the message, Romero shed his apron, revealing a gun at his side, then strode two steps back, turned, and hustled toward the scene.

Aileen produced a peppermint and told me it might help. I didn't argue. At this point, I appreciated anything to ease my cough…and nerves.

"I've fond memories of meeting you at Cynthia's wedding," she said. "What a vision of beauty ye were—and are." She patted my hand. "I thought that son of mine has finally found his match."

I warmed at her words, feeling slightly better about my situation with Romero. Maybe I'd give him some slack for not telling me he was back. It did sound like it was a last-minute plan.

Before our talk got too deep, a guy stopped at Aileen's booth for two panzerottis. In the background, an EMS truck and a fire truck sped across a vacant part of the field toward the pond, followed by several cruisers with their sirens wailing. The cruisers pulled to a stop behind the fire truck and formed a border around the scene. The victim was dead and there was no one in danger, but the Rueland police came in with their guns blazing.

A sick feeling persisted in my stomach from today's incident. If I were smart, I'd forget about the whole thing. But something told me this wasn't a simple drowning. Was it the quarrel Woody had had with Malton MacGregor? The fact his drowning was staged at the multicultural fair? The welt on his head? The mood ring on his finger?

Once Aileen's customer left with his panzerottis and two Cokes, I asked if there was anything else she remembered from last night.

She shook her head no. "Ye might want to talk to Barn MacTavish. He's in charge of the Scottish booth this year." She tightened the apron around her waist. "I'm always torn about helping there since I know many of the clans. But I married an Italian, and it's a big part of who I am." She leaned in and gave me another wink. "And I *do* make the best panzerottis in Rueland."

I smiled at that, then decided to follow her suggestion to talk to Barn MacTavish. Sure, I could've heeded Romero's warning and kept my nose out of this, but where was the sense in that?

Chapter 3

I excused my way through the carefree mob that either hadn't heard of the drowning or hadn't cared. Not surprising. At the moment, a Swiss yodeler had everyone's attention.

Shoot. I still hadn't found my parents' booth, and I couldn't call them since they didn't have cell phones. My parents lived in the 21st century when it came to most things. They had a laptop, internet, and GPS. Why getting cell phones was a big issue, I'd never know. If I didn't spot them on my way to talk to Barn MacTavish, I'd catch up with them later.

I was walking along the outskirts of the crowd, keeping my eyes peeled for either the Scottish or Armenian booth, when I had the distinct feeling I was being watched. More than watched. Assessed. Scrutinized.

I took a casual glance over my shoulder, telling myself I was being ridiculous. People got these feelings all the time in crowds. Everyone stared at everyone. At a colorful event like this, more so than usual. No need to get panicky.

I glanced over my other shoulder for good measure. But there were no familiar faces. No inquisitive expressions. And no one hiding under a black cloak, resembling the Grim Reaper. Just our friendly globe mascot, bopping around, waving at everyone it passed. Swell. It was all in my head. I had to remain cool.

Five feet from the Scottish canopy, the crowd opened up, and I all but tripped in front of Officer Martoli—Rueland's own donut-eating, smartass flatfoot—who was talking to three men at the booth, a pen and notebook in hand.

The first man was a strawberry blond and extremely large with shaggy brows and a bulbous nose. The second man was average in size, good-looking in an arrogant way, and had a cigarette dangling from his lips. Malton MacGregor? Romero's portrayal of the guy had me thinking he was a smoker. The third man had the art of scowling perfected. He seemed less confident, edgy.

All three were in kilts of different colors, and only the first man seemed interested in anything Martoli had to say. He had his hand on Martoli's shoulder in a friendly gesture.

I ducked and diverted my gaze to a glass refrigerated case, feigning interest in a couple of one-pound logs of haggis. But I wasn't fast enough to escape Martoli's scrutiny.

"There she is now," he said. "Miss Valentine Beaumont."

I cringed, waiting for the next words out of his mouth, but when I peered up at him, he had his arm out, waving me over with his pen.

What? No ball-buster jokes? No don't-get-testes-on-us remarks? No reference to my ill-famed perm-rod apprehension that left the crook, a.k.a. Ziggy Stoaks, with the voice of a choirboy? I straightened. Didn't Martoli have his Wheaties today?

I strode over, waiting for the other shoe to drop.

"You ever want a crime solved," he said to the large man, "this is the woman to see." He gave me a critical eye, wagging his pen in my face. "That's not an invitation to go poking around. Though I know everything spells murder to you."

"A-heh." What else could I say? He knew me better than I knew myself.

The big guy seemed duly impressed. "Ye mean to say you're a wee replica of Agatha Christie?"

The other two men had dubious looks on their faces. Not the least bit in awe.

"Ha! You mean Sherlock Holmes." Martoli slapped his notebook in his palm, making me jump. "You've never seen a sleuth in action until you've seen Valentine. Just stay out of her way when she starts flinging razors."

Klunk. The other shoe.

"We'll be in touch if we have more questions." Martoli shook the giant's hand, nodded at me and the other two who'd backed away, then aimed for the field.

We watched him stroll away, the big guy first to speak. "He's a bit of a blether, isn't he?"

"Pardon?" I looked past his round nose into his gray eyes, the corners carved with years of laugh lines.

"A chatterbox," he explained. "A gabber. I'm sure he means well. Just not as reserved as most cops I know."

That about summed up Martoli.

He hung his head, the laugh lines around his eyes shadowed with grief. "The wee man brought us horrible news."

While *I* may have been described as *wee*, I'd never heard anyone refer to Martoli as that. But coming from a man this guy's size, I suppose most people *were* wee.

"The drowning," I said.

"Aye. Of our friend Woody MacDunnell." He adjusted his kilt, giving me a wary look. "You knew Woody?"

"No." I gestured to the pond. "I was watching the caber toss when we discovered the…mishap."

"Mishap, my arse," the scowler muttered from ten feet away, mumbling a couple other phrases, his brogue so thick I couldn't make out a word he said. He focused his glower on the egotistical Scotsman before turning his back.

"That's Hoagy MacEwen," the giant said. "Our resident downer, so he is. And over there, smoking his brains out, is Malton MacGregor."

Of course. Malton took a drag on his cigarette and walked away, barely acknowledging I was standing there. He may have had good looks, but he lacked basic etiquette.

I gazed from Malton back to Hoagy. I wasn't sure what the dynamics were between those two, but I sensed tension on Hoagy's part.

Goliath extended his bear paw. "And I'm MacTavish. But you can call me Barn."

He certainly was built like a barn. He extended his hand, and I winced, expecting to be crushed by the mere size of his grasp. But it was warm and gentle, signifying to me Barn was also warm and gentle. *Oy*. Now I was starting to think like Max, judging people solely on looks.

Conversely, I reflected on Hoagy and Malton's rude behavior. Barn said Woody had been their friend. Strange way for friends to react. Or maybe their problem was me entering the scene, given my "flinging razors" history.

Since the other buffoon had disappeared, now was a good time to ask the scowler some questions. Not sure he'd appreciate me using his first name, and already forgetting his last, I read the moniker on the back of his T-shirt. "Excuse me, Mr. Mac…uh…E-wen. Did you see something suspicious that might've led to Woody's death?"

I received a growl in response.

"Lass." Barn patted my shoulder in a tender manner. "It's pronounced Mac-*Ewen*. Take no heed of him. We all want to find out what happened to Woody."

If that was so, then why did I have a feeling there was more to Hoagy's rancor than grieving over Woody's death? Not that I'd understand anything he had to say. But his attitude spoke volumes. He muttered some more, then went over to help a kid buying a Scottish flag-motif ball cap.

I pictured the cops working the scene, then faced Barn. "I don't want to upset anyone, but suppose it's discovered that Woody didn't drown. That it was murder. Do you know anyone who might've been on the outs with him?

Someone who may have wanted him dead?"

Barn shook his large head, going along with my questions. "Woody did seem preoccupied lately. As locals, we play football—or soccer to you—every Wednesday night, and this week he was having trouble concentrating."

My gaze wandered to Hoagy. "Do the others play as well?"

He followed my gaze. "Ye mean MacEwen and MacGregor? Aye, they're keeners."

I thought about this and suddenly visualized the welt on Woody's head. "Since Woody's mind wasn't on the game, did he get blindsided? Soccer's a rough sport."

"So it is. But Woody didn't get hurt. He was naturally talented on the field." He glanced over his shoulder and leaned down. "In the bedroom, too. But that was his business."

Hmm. Sounded like Woody was a player. Or was I jumping the gun? "Was he married?"

"Ha. Too busy for that. He was in the condo business with Pandi Gupta. Making his millions."

Pandi Gupta? I had a vague recollection of hearing that name before.

Barn must've noted the inquisitive look on my face because he raised his bear paws before I had a chance to pry further. "You're a bonnie lassie, and I'm sure ye mean well, but I cannae tell ye anything else about Woody. He really kept to himself."

I sighed louder than I intended. Why was I getting worked up anyway? Romero was on the case. He'd determine if Woody's drowning was accidental. I peered up at Barn through my lashes, giving a small smile.

"Now don't look at me with those doe eyes of yours." He hiked his thumb over his shoulder and gave his head a tilt. "Ye want to find out more about Woody, gaun yersel' and talk to Pandi. He's holding down the Indian fort, so to speak."

"Pandi's here?" I looked around. "At the fair?"

"Aye. Follow the smell of curry, and you'll find the wee man."

If I wanted to learn anything more about Woody, I had no choice. I thanked Barn and headed in the direction he'd pointed. I ventured twelve yards, deliberating on everything that had happened since I arrived at the park, when a tingle wove its way up my spine followed by the same feeling I was being watched. I did another quick surveillance of the area but came up empty. Much more of this, and I was going to need my head examined.

I shook off the weird feeling and carried on in search of Pandi. I was picking up on the curry scent when Max ran up to me, out of breath.

"I've been looking for you!" he gasped, wiping his forehead. "It's Phyllis."

I blinked at him. "What about Phyllis?"

"She's—"

Without warning, a shrill voice roared from behind, cutting him off.

I leaped a foot in the air and whirled around to face Miss Lucifer herself, Candace Needlemeyer, my archrival since beauty school.

I put a hand to my chest to calm myself and ogled Candace in her Bavarian barmaid outfit. Her siliconed boobs were pushed up to her chin, her blond hair was braided over both ears, and a tray of mini beer steins balanced in her hand.

"Valentine Beaumont," she sang, the venom in her voice snakelike.

Candace never could get enough jollies tormenting the clients in beauty school. Therefore, she'd turned her wrath on me. Her evildoings started with small pranks like painting a mustache on my mannequin, then progressed to snipping my flat-iron cord and pouring bleach in my bag. When I graduated, I bought a sturdier bag and thought I was rid of her rottenness. But a month after I opened Beaumont's, she hung a sign for Supremo Stylists three blocks away.

"Candace," I said by way of hello since I didn't speak serpent. *Aha.* That prickly feeling of being watched. *Candace.* Probably skulking around the park, waiting to pounce in her five-inch pumps and over-the-knee stockings. Genghis Khan could've taken lessons from this shrew.

Max was so dumbfounded by her presence, he forgot all about Phyllis. "I didn't know Hitler's family was having a reunion." He snatched a mini stein off Candace's tray and downed the contents. "*Prost.*"

She swung the tray away from Max, sloshing the frothy brews about. "These aren't for you, you simpleton. And I'm not related to Hitler."

"His wife, Eva Braun?" Max bid.

"Guess again, you moron."

Max grinned at me like he could do this all day. I gave him a *hold off* look. There had to be a good reason why Candace was here breathing the same air.

She shifted her gaze to me, her demeanor smug, her perfectly shadowed eyebrows arched into her hairline. "I walked by the pond earlier and what did I learn? Miss Scrotum Slayer unearthed another dead body."

You couldn't pull the wool over Candace's eyes.

"It's been months since you've been in the news," she went on. "Did you think a drowned man would be the perfect date?"

"Ha. Ha." *Witch.*

Max squinted daggers at her. "Actually, we heard he was one of *your* dates." He angled toward me. "And after meeting Candace, he threw himself in the water, deciding life wasn't worth living."

Candace puckered her lips. "I heard that, you dweeb."

"Oh," Max countered. "I thought your ears were plugged from those fat braids covering them."

She had a white-knuckled grip on the beer tray. "And to think I almost hired you as an employee. Hmph."

"I never would've worked for you," Max quipped. "I couldn't have kept up with the rabies shots."

Black smoke curled out of Candace's ears, and I thought, *diversion, before it gets ugly*. My gaze flitted past several booths and settled on the Scottish canopy. "I met some thirsty Scotsmen back there." I pointed to their stand. "Why don't you cheer them up with a mug of beer?" Ha. What could remotely cheer up Hoagy MacEwen? Meeting Candace would serve him right.

"Maybe I will," she bristled.

We watched her flounce away, then I whacked Max in the gut. "What happened to Phyllis?"

He doubled over. "*Yow!* What'd you do that for?"

I helped him uncurl. "Sorry. I guess I'm on edge. Spotting another corpse. Seeing Romero after all this time. Learning who the victim was." I pondered my next words. "Meeting his so-called friends. Discovering there was something bothering him."

I glared at the Scottish stand where Candace was waving her tray in a fetching manner. "Bumping into the antichrist was the straw that broke the camel's back."

Max rubbed his belly. "True. Candace *is* the antichrist. Apology accepted." He signaled toward the action at the pond. "Who was the victim? And what was troubling him?"

"Woody MacDunnell was his name. And I don't know the answer to your second question. But Barn MacTavish, the man working the Scottish booth, said Woody was in the condo business."

Max widened his eyes. "Barn? As in, where horses sleep and hay and grain are kept?"

"Yes. He's big...as a barn. And he said Woody was in business with Pandi Gupta." I waited a second until I was certain Max was paying attention.

"Go on," he insisted. Like he didn't appreciate me breaking this down into bite-sized bits.

"Gupta happens to run the Indian stall here at the festival. Since he had a joint venture with Woody, I'm hoping he can shed light on what was bugging the guy."

"Pandi Gupta." Max enunciated the name slowly. Then again quickly.

"Yes. Do you know him?"

"No. I just like saying his name. Pandi Gupta. Pandi Gupta."

Oh Lord. *This* for being friends with an incessant wiseass. Then again, why was I surprised? Max's interest wasn't about cultural differences. He once had a client named Merrilee Moffat. Said her name had a melodic ring to it. Proved it by singing *Merrilee Moffat* all day long.

"It's like I should be acquainted with his name," I said, "but I can't pull from memory where I've heard it before."

"Pandi Gupta. Pandi Gupta," Max rehearsed. "You're right. It's familiar to me, too."

"Maybe because you've said it a dozen times."

We walked on, and I spied the medical examiner's vehicle parked next to the fire truck. Then I recalled the wet ground and the mood ring caked to my heel.

I tipped up my shoe, confirming there was no more mud stuck to it, then explained to Max about the ring. "Did you notice anything fly off Woody's finger when he landed next to me?"

Max looked at me like my lashes weren't the only things that were squirrelly. "Lovey, I was too busy running for cover to notice jewelry showering from a cadaver."

He did a full body shiver at that, then grabbed my hand and pulled me forward. "Can we not talk about the corpse or Pandi Gupta anymore? There's another catastrophe calling for your attention…and her name is Phyllis."

Chapter 4

Max being Max, he might not want to talk about the death, but he did want to talk about the mood ring. What color was it when I found it? What shade was it on my finger? When I handed it to Romero?

I caught him between breaths. "Enough. What happened to Phyllis?"

He kept his stride. "She had a heart attack."

"*What?*" Out of reflex, I clouted him again in the stomach.

"*Owww!*" He doubled over. "What have you been doing? Lifting weights?"

I ignored his question. "What do you mean *Phyllis had a heart attack*? When?"

He took a gulp of air and leveled himself, stepping a safe distance away from me. "After she hoisted that lumber into the lake."

"Pond," I corrected.

"Whatever. I think it was too much for her."

We picked up our pace to a jog. A minute later we were inside the first-aid tent, searching for Miss Caber Toss herself.

"There she is!" Without thinking, I whacked Max again.

He gasped like he'd given up, then slapped his hands to his sides and followed my steps.

Phyllis sat on a table, her blouse loosened, a blood-pressure cuff around her arm, her hair springing every which way under her tam. The nurse tending Phyllis gave her a frazzled smile, removed the cuff, and indicated to us she was free to go.

I took Phyllis's clammy hand and smoothed it in my palm. True, she was a pain in the butt, a horrible stylist, and one of those relatives no one ever talked about. But I didn't want to see anything terrible happen to her. "How do you feel, Phyllis?"

She gave an arduous breath. "Like a brick shithouse."

"She asked how you feel, dearie," Max said, "not how you look."

I stared at Max. "You do realize you just paid her a compliment."

He jerked his head back. "You mean a woman having the physique of a defensive lineman is in vogue?"

Oh brother. Death. Divorce. Injuries. Didn't matter. You could always count on Max to make light of a bad situation. I wasn't sure what that said about him, but he lived up to the reputation. "You better go look up your idioms."

He whipped out his phone, and I concentrated on Phyllis.

Color slowly returned to her face, yet her spirits seemed low. "After I chucked that log in the pond, I felt kind of woozy." She gave an exaggerated sigh that usually garnered sympathy. "And everyone was so interested in that guy who flew out of the water. Nobody cared I was having chest pains."

"That guy drowned, Phyllis." I kept my voice gentle, figuring she wasn't aware of the outcome.

"In other words," Max added, abandoning his search, "he had a worse day than you."

Phyllis looked at him, perplexed. "All the more reason to help the living then, right?"

Max gaped at me, lost for words.

"Good thing Jock came to my rescue," she said.

My ears perked up. "Jock?"

"Yeah. He carried me here."

I took a benign glance around the tent. Phyllis's nurse was talking to a handful of festivalgoers. Another nurse was using a stethoscope on an older man. A third nurse sat at a makeshift desk. No Argentinean Hercules in sight.

Why was I surprised? Jock had been a navy fireman and ranked as master-at-arms before falling into stunt-doubling—which at times he still did between working at the shop. He'd repeatedly put out fires—figuratively speaking—and came and went like lightning.

"Where is he now?" A poker face accompanied my off-the-cuff remark.

"Beats me." Phyllis was no dummy. She'd seen the chemistry between Jock and me. Called me on it several times.

"So he's not in the park?"

She grunted. "Do I look like his keeper? Said he had somewhere to go."

Natch. Thor swoops in with the injured, leaves her in good hands, and soars off into the sunset. I doubt there was a cape adequate to fit that man.

This day kept getting better and better. Bad enough there'd been a suspicious drowning in the park, Phyllis to worry about, and Candace coloring my day, but now I had Jock's mysterious whereabouts pestering me.

"Maybe I shouldn't have lifted that caber after all." Phyllis's frown was heartbreaking. "I mean, I'm not built like a man."

A high-pitched titter came from Max, but he caught my dirty look, then squelched it.

Phyllis sounded so downtrodden, I widened my eyes at him, urging words of encouragement while throwing in a watch-what-you-say glare.

Max dumped his phone in his pocket and offered Phyllis a cheery smile. "You're as strong as an ox, remember, Phyll? How was anyone supposed to know you were having a heart attack?"

I thunked my bag on the ground. Not the encouragement I was looking for.

Phyllis fixed her blouse and hopped off the bed. "I didn't have a heart attack. They believe it was indigestion. Probably from this morning's donuts. Wait till Friar Tuck's hears about this." She adjusted her tam on an angle, then tugged down her kilt. "I've got to get back to my post. That customer might be back for the Walkman."

"You know…" Max's brows went up with his voice. "I saw the guy circling your table. Better hurry."

Phyllis charged out of the first-aid tent, and I mouthed *You're incorrigible* to Max.

"*What!*" He had his palms up, his handsome cheeks dimpled in innocence. "You wanted to cheer her up, didn't you?"

At times, Max's logic was warped. Then again, we were often on the same page, given his reasonings by and large had merit.

Since Phyllis had dodged a bullet and seemed her old self, there was the matter of talking to Pandi Gupta about his association with Woody.

We were on our way out of the tent when we collided with my mother and Tantig, my father's aunt. My mother has a Ukrainian background, but she was clothed like Tantig, layered in traditional Armenian wear with beads on their tops and scarf-type hats on their heads. Sporting glum expressions, they looked like they'd just wandered off the boat from the old country.

Alarm bells went off in my head, and a sick feeling struck my gut. Because I hadn't shown up at their booth, I'd left them shorthanded. Something awful must've happened.

"What are you two doing here?" I gave Tantig a warm squeeze, trying to sound lighthearted. "Who's watching the booth?"

My mother lifted my great-aunt's hand wrapped in a tea towel. "Tantig sliced her thumb making tabbouleh. I think she may need stitches." She gave a grim exhale.

"And your father's managed to put down his cigar for twenty minutes to work the booth."

She slanted closer and creased her eyebrows at me. "What's that on your eyes? Looks like black thread."

Right when I was beginning to forget about these saggy lashes. Feeling the left one had loosened again, I pressed the outer corner hard, until I saw spots. "They're false eyelashes."

My mother straightened. "Why are you wearing false eyelashes? You've got the longest, thickest lashes I've ever seen."

"That's what *I* said," Max piped.

I stared Max down, then veered my attention back to my mother. "Salesmen sometimes leave me stuff to try. I'm simply testing them."

My mother shook her head, like *What next?* "Sheila Kunkel's daughter had such a time with false eyelashes. She ripped out her own lashes trying to get the damned things off."

"Mom, can we get back to Tantig's hand? Let me see the cut." As a hairstylist, I'd given my knuckles so many gashes, I could recognize the severity of a wound faster than a surgeon.

Without waiting for permission, I unwrapped the towel from Tantig's hand and examined the cut. Thankfully, the slice wasn't as bad as I expected. "Are you okay, Tantig?"

My great-aunt rolled her eyes in her classic inflated manner. "Your mother thinks I'm dy-ink." Her words were slow and thickly accented, her tone lifeless.

My mother sighed as if it were her God-given right to worry over the woman. Truth was, having recently moved Tantig into their home, my mother could've won caretaker of the year. She shifted Tantig's patent leather purse under her arm. "Tell me again, are you in pain?" She massaged my great-aunt's uninjured hand while pumping for information.

"I'll give you a Tic Tac if you stop fuss-ink over me." Tantig was a fan of Tic Tacs, soap operas, and weather channels. She wasn't a fan of being coddled.

The nurse hurried from around the desk, sat Tantig in a chair, and produced gauze and antiseptic. "There's a doctor on call, but after they found that body by the pond, he rushed out to see if there was anything he could do."

My mother swung her head so rapidly from the nurse to me, her dangling scarf swept her in the face. She swiped the scarf back, her eyes laser sharp. "Tell me you don't know what she's talking about, Valentine."

I smiled innocently, hoping she saw the halo above my head. "I don't know what she's talking about."

"Is that why you didn't show up at our tent today? You exposed another dead body?"

Max squeaked. "Time to go now."

"I didn't exactly expose it." No sense sharing it was Phyllis's doing.

The nurse quickly cleaned and wrapped a bandage around Tantig's thumb, then packed up her things and got the hell out of Dodge before it got ugly. Smart woman.

My mother was still scrutinizing me as the nurse scurried away. "You know your nose twitches when you lie?"

Max's jaw dropped to his knees. "I once told her the same—"

I elbowed Max hard in the ribs, this time fully aware of my actions.

He *oofed*, and I made a nonchalant expression to my mother, resisting the urge to clasp my nose. "It does not." It twitched when I was nervous or scared. Neither of which I was going to admit.

My mother stood there, waiting for an explanation. Tantig sat in her chair, staring straight ahead, probably wishing she were in front of a TV with her favorite stars.

"I don't know any more than you." I shrugged. "Just that a body of a man was found by the pond earlier. Would it make you feel better if I said a corpse sailed out of the water like a missile and plummeted by my feet?" I gave a short laugh to show the absurdity of it.

My mother was on to me. "Who was the man? Anyone we know?"

Oh boy. "His name was Woody MacDunnell. He was part of the Scottish clan groups that are here."

"Was he murdered?"

"Mom, do I look like a detective?"

She did a once-over from my head to my heels. "No. But you don't look like an amateur sleuth either. And guess who keeps solving crimes like Jessica Fletcher?"

I stifled a smile at her backhanded compliment. "If you're going to compare me to anyone, I'd rather it be Angelina Jolie in *Lara Croft: Tomb Raider*. We have the same hair."

She tapped her fingers on Tantig's purse, not amused.

"Well?" I squawked. "Romero's on the case. Let's see what he reveals."

"That's never stopped you before from getting involved."

She had me there. "I wasn't even here last night when everyone was setting up, assuming that's the last anyone saw of Woody."

"We were here. I don't recall any hullabaloo." She tapped the purse again, a contemplative look crossing her face. "There was one gentleman, though, from the Scottish booth who was flirting with Tantig." She handed my great-aunt her purse. "Remember, Tantig? He was in a kilt and had a beard and clipped haircut except for a patch of brown wave on top. He passed our stall and gave you a wink."

Whoa. Woody MacDunnell to a *T*. Barn had even insinuated he was a ladies' man. Not sure what he thought he was achieving, flirting with an eighty-year-old woman. But maybe he was being courteous to someone whom he thought deserved kindness.

"Who-hk cares?" Tantig rolled her eyes again. Likely not impressed with my mother's storytelling. Moreover, she didn't like being the center of attention.

I crouched in front of my great-aunt. "Did you see the man again, Tantig?"

She nodded, her dull stare aimed past my shoulder. "By the bathroom."

My mother shook her head at Tantig. "The bathrooms are being refurbished, remember? You had to use the porta potty behind our booth."

Tantig winched up her chin and gave a *tsk*. Like *Don't remind me.* I couldn't blame her. I didn't want to be a snob about it, but I'd hold it in before I ever stepped foot in a porta potty.

"I saw that globe, too."

"The mascot?" I wanted to hear what Tantig knew about Woody, and she was naming off things she spotted in the park.

"Can you remember what time you saw Woody?" I asked. "Was it seven o'clock? Eight?"

"I don't know." She heaved a heavy sigh, likely wishing we'd stop probing. "The door was stuck, and I couldn't get in. The man reached past me and opened the door for me." She shifted her uninterested gaze to me. "That's when I saw the ring on his fing-air."

"Ring?"

"It had a red gem," she said in her monotone.

The mood ring.

"Red?" I asked. "You're sure it wasn't green or purple or blue?"

My mother looked at me like I had a screw loose. "Tantig may be elderly, dear, but she knows her colors." She studied me with fresh eyes. "Why the interest in a ring? Does this have something to do with the murder?"

Listen to her. Angela Lansbury herself.

"Nobody said it was murder. Woody MacDunnell was wearing a mood ring last night, but the colors were different." I ruminated on this for a moment, Max and my mother gawking at me.

"*What?*"

My mother gestured *come on* with her hand. "How do you know the colors were different?"

"Oh. That." Disregarding Max's shrewd expression since he already knew the truth, I centered on my mother's puzzled face. "Romero's mother noticed Woody's ring last night during the coffee break." Acting blasé, I waved toward the tent's exit. "With so many vendors here, and people coming and going, you probably didn't see them."

New hope registered on my mother's face, the ring totally forgotten. "Romero's mother? She's here at the festival?"

Think, Valentine. Think. My mother had briefly met Romero on the Love Boat this past fall. Last thing I needed was for her to descend on his mother, hoping to plan showers and order wedding corsages.

"She *was* here," I said, "but I think she's gone now."

"Gone? Where?"

"Uh, back to Italy."

My mother's face fell a few degrees. "Oh. That's too bad. I would've liked to meet her."

"Yes, that would've been great." I snapped my fingers at the misfortune of it all. "Another time."

I avoided Max's chiding look. I knew what he was thinking, but I had to derail my mother somehow. I put that out of my mind and reviewed Tantig's story. By spotting Woody's ring glowing red, she must've seen him before dark.

"He was in no hurry to leave," Tantig finished.

Say what? Why would he hang around the toilets? "Did you see or hear anything when you were in the porta potty?"

"I heard him arguing with another person."

I looked from Max to my mother, eyes wide. "With a man or a woman?"

Tantig shrugged and lowered her lids to half-mast, signaling she was about done playing Twenty Questions.

I patted her knee. "Tantig?"

She blinked at me. "It was too muffled to tell."

Wait a minute. Aileen heard him bickering with Malton MacGregor last night. But didn't she say it was when they were leaving the park? Maybe it was around the same time that Tantig had seen Woody. Or shortly after, and the dispute between the two had escalated.

Out of the blue, my mind shifted to the scowler, Hoagy MacEwen, and his *Mishap, my arse* comment regarding Woody's drowning. It could've been grief talking, but something told me he knew more. "Could you tell if the person had an accent?"

Tantig shook her head no. And the more I thought about it, an accent could be turned on and off. Scottish-born actor Gerard Butler had proven that. Granted, I hadn't heard Malton MacGregor speak, but it was worth noting.

"If this doesn't spell murder," my mother chimed, "I don't know what does."

It was too soon to tell, and I had no proof, but I had a creeping sensation she was right. My mother. The woman who reamed me out every time I stepped foot in a murder investigation. Were times changing? Had she finally come to grips with my sleuthing side?

I wasn't going to stand around pondering that miracle any further. Something suspicious was going on at the multicultural fair. *Lara Croft: Tomb Raider* or not. I could feel it.

Maybe Woody MacDunnell's death hadn't been declared murder. And maybe my imagination was in typical overdrive. But how could my hometown be under the scrutiny of another possible homicide? And if it *was* homicide, how would I find answers to my questions if I didn't keep snooping?

Chapter 5

Max and I aimed in the direction of the international booths. I picked up on the curry smell again while he preached about how I talked to my mother.

"She just wants to keep you safe." He wagged his finger in front of my nose.

I slapped his hand away and hitched my bag higher up my shoulder. "Is it my fault dead bodies keep landing in my path?" I mulled this over some more, the mood ring coming to mind. "It's like I'm cursed. Maybe the colors on the ring were trying to tell me something." Which reminded me. I had to call my best friend, Twix. Not only was she a mother of two with a thriving daycare and a devoted husband, but she could find an explanation for any story. She'd be an expert at this.

"Yeahhh. You should look into it. I know! Why don't you go to a psychic or a fortune teller?" He scanned the park, clasping his hands in glee. "I bet there's a fortune teller already set up here."

I was about to respond to his silly suggestion when we spotted the medical examiner and the other emergency units leaving the scene. A cloud of dust flew up around the vehicles, and like a mirage, Romero with his sexy gait sauntered toward us through the haze.

He looked every bit the rugged movie star, clad in his

tight jeans, denim shirt, and gun at his side. Knowing a hard-muscled body throbbing with life was underneath the clothes caused a huge lump in my throat.

Holy Toledo. I swallowed past the lump. Max was right. How could I resist Romero? He was sexy and dangerously handsome. Not that I needed to be told that. Someone with cataracts could see Romero was a gorgeous specimen.

Max clutched my arm and used it to smack himself in the stomach.

I wrestled my arm away. "What are you doing?"

"Thought I'd save you the energy." A sigh escaped his lips, and he got all dreamy-eyed.

"Get a grip." Silently, I agreed with his take on Romero. If there was one person on earth who could melt me with his presence, it was this man. Okay, Jock had also been known to have the power to condense me to a gushy puddle, but there it was. Valentine Beaumont, Miss Vulnerable. Swept away by two hot men. If I didn't get control of my emotions, soon Betty and Birdie's friend Emery would melt me with his dimply Winnie-the-Pooh smile.

"Well?" Romero stopped in front of us, hands on hips, stern gaze fixed on me.

My muscles tingled, and my legs almost gave out from beneath me. "Well?" I wasn't going to appear anxious. I matched his gaze, his prolonged eye contact making me hot while simultaneously unnerving me. This couldn't be good.

Out of the corner of my eye, I saw Max bobbing his head from Romero to me, the heat between us so strong even Max felt its intensity. "Um, should I vanish?"

Romero arched a brow at the suggestion, the racy gleam in his eye not getting by me.

I wanted to shout *Yes!* and jump Romero's bones. I wanted to pick up where we'd left off several months ago. To feel his rough jaw against my skin, his toned hands circling my breasts, his full mouth sweeping across my flesh. The gleam in Romero's eye turned penetrating.

No mistaking. If Max hadn't been here, Romero would've thrown me to the ground and straddled me on all fours, tormenting me with erotic kisses till I begged for more.

A stirring moved straight from my shoulders to my belly and traveled south. Damn, I just knew my face was reddening, too.

Ding-dong, a little voice cried in my head. *This isn't the time or place for romantic play. A body's been found in the park. Get real.*

Heeding the voice, I breathed deeply and refocused on the here and now. Romero had news on the case. I could sense it.

He got right to it. "The ME discovered multiple bruises on the body and two contusions on the skull." He indicated to the back of his head. "One on the occipital bone, the other at the temple where you noticed the bump. The bruises on the body, at this point, could be from anything, even from the canoe that it was trapped under. The contusions on the skull are another matter."

He inhaled through his nose, looked from Max to me, then exhaled and shook his head, leaving out *here we go again*. "Unless the victim did a backward dance into a tree, then threw himself into the pond, we're looking at murder."

My conversation with Barn came to mind. "Woody played soccer once a week. Maybe the bruises on his body were from a typical game." Barn claimed Woody didn't get blindsided the last time he played, but with all the kicking and shoving in soccer, you had to expect a few bruises here and there.

Romero's eyebrow went up. "May I inquire how you know this? Wait. Forget I asked."

I puffed out air. "You don't need to get surly about it. I merely talked to Barn MacTavish at the Scottish booth."

I could see the wheels turning in his head. After all, I'd talked to Barn *before* Woody's death had officially been declared murder. "Before you say anything, our earlier chat had me curious about Woody. Since he was wearing a kilt,

I figured no harm talking to the people at the Scottish stall."

Romero crossed his arms and raised his right hand to scratch the dark stubble on his chin. "A casual interest, one might say…like the one you had about the mood ring."

"Precisely!" I knew he was being sarcastic, but I faked gusto.

"Well?" He motioned with his hand to tell him more. "Did you learn anything else from…Barn?"

I gave him a steely-eyed look, then got over myself. "Actually, yes. Woody had a reputation with women. And not that this was spoken, but there seemed to be dissension between Woody and the other men at the Scottish booth."

"What do you mean, dissension?"

"I'm not sure, but there was no love lost over his death."

Romero dropped his chin a notch. "You got all this from a few minutes talking to Barn."

"Yes. Martoli was there. He can verify what I heard."

He deliberated on this. "What about Malton MacGregor? Did you talk to him?"

"No." Romero's take on MacGregor seemed accurate. He was an ignorant sod and had a shifty manner. I didn't know what his run-ins with the law were about, and I didn't like to pass judgment on someone I hardly knew, but he was a man I didn't want to be alone with. "He did, however, snub me with precision and arrogance."

Romero gave me a razor-sharp glare that zinged to my soul. "Stay away from him. The guy's corrupt. I don't trust him."

"Don't worry. I have no plans of coming within two feet of him." Ten feet, maybe, but all things considered, probably not something I should convey to Romero.

He rolled his eyes like he wished the day was done, then paused, clearly debating how much more to divulge. "Judging from the greenish cast to the body, the marbling in the veins, and the miniscule amount critters fed off the bloated corpse, time of MacDunnell's death was last night, not long after dark."

That much had to be true. Sealed by the fact that we already knew he'd been wearing his kilt last night during setup. Trying not to let the gross details affect my stomach, I sucked in air, organized my thoughts, then relayed Tantig's story about seeing Woody at the porta potty. Plainly one of the last to witness him alive.

Before Romero gave me his challenging look or another zing to the soul, I professed Tantig's story came out innocently.

He did another head shake that said, Why do I bother?

I shifted my gaze, briefly distracted from Romero, to the globe mascot, tripping over its big feet while strolling by.

Romero glimpsed toward the exit where the emergency vehicles departed. "They're taking the body back to the morgue for more analysis. If we're right and death was caused by trauma to the head, according to the size and shape of the contusions, the murder weapon was a flat, blunt instrument."

I pictured Woody's algae-covered body dislodging from the canoe before it flew my way. "As in a canoe paddle?"

He did a *comme-ci-comme-ça* shrug. "It's possible, but there's no paddle in sight. The sheriff's office is giving us a hand with a dive team. Short of dragging the pond for evidence, it's our best course of action to find a murder weapon."

Max, who'd been absorbing every word, took a cautious glance around the grounds. "So there could be a murderer in the park? At this very moment?"

One of Romero's strengths as a detective was his ability to remain cool, unrushed. He widened his stance and centered on Max. "Could be. Sometimes a killer delights in witnessing the find, watching things unfold. Then again, he or she may be long gone." He motioned behind him. "The area's been cordoned off. Divers'll be here soon. In the meantime, the team's doing a ground search."

He tipped his head at me. "Maybe locate a canoe paddle. We'll also be conducting more interviews."

"A job Martoli appears to enjoy," I reported.

Romero grinned. "Gotta love that guy. He thrives on preliminaries. Likes to see what he can dig up."

Yeah, like old jokes that should be laid to rest.

As if reading my thoughts, Romero dropped the smile, stepped past Max, and wrapped one arm around my waist. "And *you*, Miss Butterfly Lashes"—he brought me up tight against his hard form, his voice low, his stubble an inch from my cheek—"I hope you remembered our last encounter, the one that dealt with self-defense and staying safe."

My pulse rushed through my veins at his words. "*Oui.*" Our last encounter was burned in my memory.

"Don't be cute. There's a maniac out there. I don't want you getting hurt." He tightened his hold on me, his finger tracing my saucy, French-speaking mouth.

Max peeped. "I think I'll be moving along now."

Resisting the urge to nip Romero's finger, I backed out of his arms and gained control, remembering there was a murder scene, an unexplained corpse, and a time and place for everything. "Does this mean you're closing down the fair?"

He took a grim look around the park. "Not at this point. We can carry on the investigation without disrupting things."

Max fiddled with his hands, the worry on his face compounding. "What if there's another murder?"

Romero nodded at him. "*Then* we'll close down the fair."

Cop humor.

He flicked the tip of my nose, said he had to go, then hustled toward a couple of uniforms. Max and I gaped from Romero to each other.

"Now what?" Max said on an exhale.

I stuck out my chest, full of confidence. "Pandi Gupta, remember?"

He swung his head from Romero's receding back, to me. "Didn't you hear the man? He said he doesn't want you getting hurt."

"Pff. He's always saying things like that." I marched toward the exhibition area, sobering inside because the truth was, Romero had once loved another woman who *had* gotten hurt. Her death had left him a hollow man, one who'd become cold, insensitive. He'd excelled at his job, but at what cost? When we'd first met, he'd been arrogant, untouchable, inhumane. I shuddered at the memory. I didn't want to resurrect those feelings again. But I also couldn't ignore the present situation. "We carry on with our investigation."

"*Our?*" Max ran up behind me and tapped my shoulder. "When did it become *our*?"

"When you professed your undying love for me."

He stopped short, his expression sly. "When did I do that?"

I stalled, searching for the right answer. "When you saved me from being flattened by that airborne cadaver."

He narrowed his gaze and couldn't have looked more like a pirate if he'd had a patch on one eye and a parrot on his shoulder. "I didn't exactly save you. Your heels stuck in the mud, remember?" He stiffened. "Anyway, I would've done the same for anyone."

While he reflected on this, I went in for the kill. "What about when you said I had the longest, thickest lashes you'd ever seen? There was love in those words." I batted my eyelashes so fast, the left one drooped over my eyeball. *Shoot.*

"Now you're getting cheeky."

I was, too.

He came toe to toe and held his index finger under my mouth, palm up. "Spit."

I jerked my head back and stared up into his dazzling greenish-brown eyes. "Why?"

"A bit of moisture will make the glue on your lashes tacky, and then we can set them in place."

Max knew every trick in the book, from saving a broken fingernail to tightening saggy jowls. Who was I to argue?

I spit on his finger, and he leaned in, moistening the outer corner of the fake lashes. Then he pinched them together with my own lashes. I blinked a few times, hoping I'd make it through the rest of the day until I could remove them in the comfort of my own home.

"Joking aside," I continued, "now that we know Woody was murdered, don't you want to get to the bottom of this? Find out who did it?"

He bit his lip, avoiding my stare. "I'm quite happy to let the police discover who did it. They're the ones with the guns, in case you hadn't noticed."

I picked up the pace again. "I noticed all right." I patted my trusty bag of tools by my side. "In case *you* hadn't noticed, I've got this."

"Uh-huh. Mary Poppins strikes again."

There was a certain ring to that that I liked. I kept up my stride in silence, a small smile planted on my face. Max, on the other hand, gave a nervous sigh, like maybe this time my bag wouldn't provide safety when I needed it.

I brushed off the sigh and remained steadfast. Fact of the matter was, someone killed Woody MacDunnell at the festival last night, leaving his body battered and bruised. On top of that, Malton MacGregor was overheard having a dispute with Woody. Tantig also heard rumblings between Woody and someone outside the porta potty.

Added to the mystery, Woody was a known ladies' man. Not to mention there was the issue of the mood ring. Trying to make sense of these things was like taming a tornado with a hair towel. Nothing added up, and the mood ring wasn't much of a clue.

Nonetheless, it wasn't in me to admit defeat. Rueland had always been a safe place to live, despite past murders. But even those had occurred in private settings. Okay, maybe not so private. But nothing compared to our beloved town park with its beautifully lit gazebos, footbridges, carved shrubs, and winding paths. The place was right out of a romance novel.

I soldiered on, determination brimming within me. My instinct said if I dug deep enough, I'd find out the truth behind Woody's demise. Nothing was going to stop me from removing this heavy cloak of doom from this magnificent landmark. With or without Max's help, I was rooted to this case until I found a murderer.

Chapter 6

Max and I were closing in on the action at the exhibition area when Candace sashayed up to us, shoulders back, beer tray absent from her hand.

"*Heil*, Frau Needlemeyer." Max saluted. "What happened? Family reunion get cut short?"

Candace gave Max the evil eye. "Aren't you a barrel of laughs." She stuck her head high. "If you must know, we're waiting for more kegs to be delivered. Can't keep up to the demand."

I watched a couple of youths strut by, bouncing empty beer steins in their palms, snickering and belching behind Candace's back.

"I hope you're asking for IDs," I said. "A lot of adolescents are here."

She sneered at me, deaf to the ruckus behind her. "What do you think I am? A numbskull? I know an underage kid when I see one."

The teens, who'd leaned in to listen, cracked up at this.

I put my palms up in surrender. "No need to get touchy. I wouldn't want you to go to jail for serving minors." Biggest lie ever. If Candace went to jail, she'd finally be off my back. And it wasn't like the concept of prison was foreign to her. Her grandpa, Two-Notes, was living out his retirement in the big house for bank robbery. Candace could make it a family affair.

"That's the problem with you, Valentine," she said, hands on hips. "You think you know everything. For your information, we have a license this weekend that covers everything. And I'm not serving to anyone I shouldn't."

"Good to know." I smiled, letting her insult run off my back. Meanwhile, the youths were making clown faces behind her head, mocking her words. "Ta-ta then. Don't get into trouble."

I took a step forward, but she blocked my path, her boobs level with my chin. "Speaking of trouble," she added, "word in the park is that the victim of the drowning was Woody MacDunnell. And it wasn't a drowning at all. It was *murder*."

"*A plus!*" Max clapped his hands. "Go to the front of the class."

Candace overlooked Max's remark and homed in on me, leaving me no choice but to stare up into her baby blues.

"You knew Woody?" I asked.

"Everyone knew Woody," she boasted. "He was a good-time guy."

Max and I exchanged a look, convinced Candace was speaking from personal experience.

According to Barn, Woody kept to himself, which could've been true. One could be a "good-time guy" and not get involved or get close to anyone in a real sense. Especially someone like Candace.

"How did you know him?" No harm in asking.

She wagged her long, red-tipped fingernail in my face. "I see what you're doing, Valentine. You're fishing for information so you can solve this case. Well, you're out of luck. You're not the only beautician who can catch a killer and make headlines. *I'm* going to find who murdered Woody MacDunnell for myself. I've got the smarts and intuition to solve any crime."

"Said the woman who served beer to minors," Max offered.

Candace huffed and flipped back one of her braids. "I'm done talking to you two comedians. If you want me, I'll be doing *real* detective work."

"*Auf Wiedersehen!*" Max chirped, watching her stalk away toward the cordoned-off crime scene. "Poor cops. They don't know what they're in for." He shook his head, then grabbed my arm. "Come on. We've got work to do."

"Pardon?" I pulled back. "A few minutes ago, you were happy to let the police solve the murder."

"That was before Miss Bavaria threw down the gauntlet." He sighed with extra emphasis. "She's as dumb as dish soap, but she may also get lucky. Which means we better get busy because I'm not going to let her show you up."

I took a second to bask in the warmth of his words. But in all honesty, a fire had already ignited inside. I wasn't one to shy away from a challenge. And if Candace thought she was going to one-up me, she was even dumber than dish soap.

Maybe this murder case was going to prove tougher than the others I'd been involved in. And perhaps I hadn't yet discovered anything worth noting. But Hercule Poirot didn't discover the murderer on the Orient Express in an afternoon. And just because Candace had a big mouth and flashy manner didn't mean she'd get the answers she was looking for.

Max waved his hand in my face and snapped his fingers. "Let's go." He ushered me toward the tents. "We've got a murder to solve."

Max stopped in his tracks in the middle of the exhibition area and did a Superman—fists on hips, legs wide—pose. "Where the heck is the tent?"

"This way." I spotted the national flag of India along another row of canopies. As we drew near the tent, a hypnotic, chanting melody from a stringed sitar and woodwind instrument became stronger.

Other sounds faded into the background and, out of nowhere, a prickle shot down my spine accompanied with that feeling I was being watched...again. Silly. The music was having an effect on me. That was all. I took a casual look around the crowd anyway.

I was positive Candace was the reason for that feeling earlier since she'd been slithering about. But she was by the pond, harassing the police. Who else would be spying on me? Malton MacGregor? MacEwen? They had a booth to run. They weren't wasting their time tracing my footsteps. If it wasn't the alluring Indian music giving me weird ideas, maybe it was the smell of curry soaking through me.

Max evidently felt a vibe from the music, too. He shivered, his eyes big and round. "I have a hunch we're about to meet Aladdin and Genie inside the magic lamp."

Trust Max to bring make-believe into it. "If you want to get technical..." I faced him. "Aladdin was from the Middle East, not India." I continued before he could interrupt. "And I don't remember the fictitious name of that Arabian city."

"Agrabah." Didn't miss a beat. "And look at the size of the tent. All the other canopies look like pup tents compared to this monstrosity. Pandi Gupta must be rolling in dough."

"I don't know. Let's find out."

The huge tent was sectioned into three smaller tents, each with its own front entrance but also interconnecting from inside. The first was the food tent where smells of curry, cumin, and cloves drifted our way. Perched behind a counter were three elderly women in colorful saris, dishing out samosas, tandoori chicken, and naan bread.

"Yum." Max patted his belly. "I could go for tandoori chicken."

I gawked from the three women to the fly tape hanging from the rafters to Max while he caught the drool escaping the corners of his mouth. "Go ahead. No need to solve a murder when there's tandoori chicken to eat."

He turned his head in slow motion and squinted at me. "Are you being sarcastic?"

"What do you think?"

"I think I'm going to tell Romero to use handcuffs on you next time he's teaching you the finer points of self-defense."

Wise guy. "Well? Are you going for chicken or what?"

He peered up at the fly tape and crinkled his nose. "I've lost my appetite. Lead the way."

We ambled into the second tent and took in the racks of fancy Bollywood dresses, beads, headpieces, ceramics, baskets, and a multitude of Indian crafts. Nowhere did I see a wee man who could've resembled Pandi Gupta. In fact, other than half a dozen festivalgoers eyeballing the goods, the only other person around was a petite woman manning the tent. She was about twenty-nine, dressed in a pink and gold sari, and she was in the far corner, folding blouses.

Max and I sauntered up to her, giving her a moment to finish what she was doing. She left the blouses, slid around a counter, and gave a client a charming smile that lit up the room.

Max gulped and froze on the spot, a look of awe filling his face. He'd worn a similar look when he'd first laid eyes on Romero, and the day I hired Jock, and every time one of Jock's gorgeous clients walked through the salon door. But this was different. The corners of his astute eyes softened, his focus unyielding, and I swore I saw his heart hammering under his shirt. My guess was love at first sight. Who could blame him? I'd never seen anyone more beguiling in my whole life.

The young woman had long black hair with impossible shine. Light brown skin the color of hazelnut chocolate. And her eyes! Mesmerizing and impossibly green, they seemed to glow from within. Added to her entrancing beauty was a pear-shaped medallion resting at the top of her forehead.

Neither one of us could take our eyes off her, but it was rude to stare. And one of us had to say something.

I backhanded Max in the stomach, spurring him on. To no avail. He was a goner.

Wonderful.

She looked our way, and I extended my hand and introduced myself…and Max.

"I'm Adia," she said.

Something in the way her smile faded and her eyebrow arched told me she'd heard about my past. Could've been paranoia on my part, but I'd been the receiver of that look too many times to discount it.

She shifted her hesitant gaze to my silent buddy. "Max?"

Max swallowed again, and it appeared his heartbeat had returned to ground level. "I'm…I'm Max."

Darn it if he didn't look cute, all tongue-tied and starry-eyed. I tapped him on the shoulder. "You've already been introduced."

He either didn't hear me or was in such a trance, nothing was getting through. That was fine by me. He could gaze at Adia all day. I was moving on. "We're looking for Pandi Gupta."

"Pandi is my father." Her English was upper crust with a subtle hint of Indian. For someone with a small stature, she reeked of confidence. "He's here somewhere." She scanned the tent. "Must've stepped out for a minute." She transferred her stare back to Max, her brows knit together. "Max? Don't you recognize me? I'm Adia. From summer camp that one year in Maine."

I blinked from Adia to Max. "Summer camp?" I had a sudden vision of Max as a little boy, building a fire and setting up camp, adding a mat to his floor and mini lights to the rafters.

Max ignored me and swooped up Adia in his arms. "I wasn't sure it was you." They hugged tightly, then went back to staring at each other. "What were we? Ten or eleven?"

She smiled up at him. "I was ten. You were going on twelve. I guess I've changed a lot since then."

"Only more beautiful." His eyes held so much adoration for this woman, I felt like I was intruding just by being there.

They joked about their days at camp, asking each other questions, forgetting I was standing three feet away.

"Uh, I hate to interrupt, but do you know when your father might be back?"

"No," Adia said, not too concerned.

"Maybe he went to see what the commotion was about at the pond."

She shrugged. "Could be. I heard it was a drowning."

"Yes." I proceeded cautiously. "That was the initial belief. But after further probing, the police are now ruling it as murder."

Her green eyes held steady on mine, the glow so powerful I almost forgot my next thought.

"Do they know who the victim was?" she asked.

"His name was Woody MacDunnell."

Her eyes widened into a beautiful almond shape. "That's terrible! Woody was my father's business partner."

She turned away to hide her expression and missed the *slap* by my head that nearly hurtled me to the top of the tent.

Slap. Slap.

"*What the*—" I whipped around and faced a thin brown man about my height, dressed in a green-and-orange sports jersey. He was gripping a fly swatter, whacking flies, shrieking obscenities.

"Dad! Stop!" Adia spun around in time to save me from being swatted. "These people would like to talk to you." She introduced us, omitting she knew Max from her youth.

Pandi lowered his fly swatter and moved closer to me. "Valentine Beaumont?" His Indian accent was thick.

"Yes." I was certain I'd never seen him before. I waited

a beat, thinking he might recognize me. All I got was a sturdy gaze from his beady eyes.

"I do apologize if I scared you." He backed up a foot and raked his fingers through his black hair. "Where there are food festivals there are flies. I do not want flies in my tent!"

"That's reasonable." I exhaled. Not only did he not recognize me, it didn't seem he'd heard of my past.

A second later, he smacked a fly on the rack beside me, making me jump again. I slid Max a questioning look, but he was still in staring-at-Adia mode.

Good grief.

"I already know what you are about to tell me, Miss Valentine." Pandi flicked the fly off the rack with his swatter. "It's about Woody. He's dead."

Guess he *had* heard of my past. "Yes." I wasn't sure where to go from here, but condolences were in order. "I'm sorry. You must be devastated."

"I am. Woody was a good friend. We had a strong partnership." He shook his head sadly, then smacked another fly with the swiftness of a frog's tongue. "I will miss him."

Was it me, or was there a disconnect between his words and his actions? Perhaps it was a cultural thing that prevented him from getting worked up over the death of a close friend.

Adia, on the other hand, had her eyes downcast and was biting her perfectly shaped lips.

"What are you going to do about it?" Pandi asked me.

"Excuse me?"

"I talked to the police. They think Woody was murdered." He pointed his fly swatter at me. "And you are that crazy lady who captures killers using hair curlers. So I would like to know what you are going to do about finding Woody's murderer."

Not that I didn't appreciate his faith in me that I could find Woody's killer, but his demanding tone was off-putting. I chalked it up to a mix of fear and concern and moved on.

"Since you asked, was there anything troubling Woody?"

He frowned and crossed his arms, the fly swatter, for once, at rest in his hand. "How do you mean?"

I thought about what I'd learned so far. "Maybe you could begin by telling me what kind of partnership you had with Woody."

"That is easy. We bought hotels. Sometimes we purchased land and developed hotels. All in all, it was a fruitful business."

I scratched my chin. Barn had said they were in the condo business. I suppose there was a correlation. "Wasn't it condominiums you bought?"

He did a distasteful *tsk* with his tongue. "I would not be bothered with such a thing. Woody and I even started a new project called Gupta's Getaways. Weekend escapes for the rich and famous." He poked his nose in my face. "Surely you have heard of this."

"No."

He looked baffled. "You do not get out much. It has been in the news. Do you not read the newspaper?"

Seemed like a rhetorical question, which was just as well. He dug into his shirt pocket. "You really need to see one of Gupta's Getaways. Here is my card. The address is on the back."

I took the card and studied the picture of an ivory-colored marble hotel. Looked like the Taj Mahal on a smaller scale.

"As for what was troubling Woody, I do not know of any such thing. He was a hard worker, and we got along famously."

"What about enemies? Did Woody ever complain he was having issues or arguments with anyone?"

Pandi pursed his lips. "Business is business. We all get into arguments. But that is part of the job. There was nothing that did not get resolved, as far as I could see."

I tucked the card in my bag. "What about on a more personal note? Perhaps with someone he was involved with."

"You are talking about someone of the female persuasion." He frowned some more, taking this line of questioning seriously.

Out of the corner of my eye, I noticed Adia step back, either giving us privacy or maintaining a safe distance from perhaps being questioned more herself.

"What Woody did on his free time, I do not know," Pandi declared.

Uh-huh.

"Now if you pardon me, I need to see those ladies about these flies." He slapped his fly swatter left and right, disappearing into the food tent.

I swiveled around to Max, but he'd approached Adia and was deep in conversation. To her credit, she brightened at Max's wit and adorable charm.

Let him have a few minutes to catch up. What could it hurt?

I moseyed around the tent, wondering again where I'd heard Pandi's name before. It hadn't been from Max. By all accounts, this was the first time he'd met the man. Maybe it simply had a melodic ring to it. Like Merrilee Moffat.

I idled by a long, glass-top jewelry counter, taking an interest in custom pieces. I ran my hands across the smooth glass, then stopped cold, coughing before I swallowed my tongue.

Staring up at me from the display case was a row of mood rings with glowing stones. Just like the mood ring Woody had worn.

My eyes got big, my throat dry. Instinctively, I wheeled around to show Max. Humph. No Max. Where'd he go?

A woman with curly blond hair sallied up beside me and eyed the rings. "Beauties, aren't they?"

I posed a hesitant smile. "Uh, yes. Popular, too."

"You're not kidding. I helped a friend set up for the fair last night and saw a guy wearing one. I figured mood rings were more for women. Not the first time I've been wrong."

I gave her a double take. "This guy you saw wearing the ring. Was he in a kilt?"

"As a matter of fact, he was. Cute, too, with a chic beard. Gave me a wink."

Mmm-hmm. Woody got around.

"Be careful, though, if you buy one and it turns black." She hushed. "Seriously, you'd be wise to watch your step. Nothing good will come your way."

Okay. Where was Max? Did he put her up to this?

I scanned the tent and brought my gaze back to the lady, but she'd wandered into the food tent, the back of her blond curls the last I saw of her before she completely disappeared.

I meandered back to the spot where I'd left Max, but he was nowhere in sight. Neither was Adia, for that matter. Of all times to take off. And without telling me.

Cutting Max some slack, I looked at the side entrance to the third tent. Yes. That had to be it. Adia was likely showing him what else they had to offer.

I hurried to the opening but didn't see Max anywhere. In fact, there was only one person in the tent, and he wasn't shopping.

Chapter 7

"Kashi?" I blinked twice, thinking my lashes were truly impairing my vision.

"It is I," my thin Indian friend from the Love Boat announced from behind a table marked "Get Out of Town Brooches."

"What are you doing here?" I couldn't believe I was standing in the same room as someone I'd once thought guilty of murder. Behind his steel-rimmed glasses, there was a wary look in his eyes as if he were thinking the same thing. Thank goodness we'd buried the hatchet.

"I am selling my brooches." He pushed up his glasses. "I make a killing on them. You do know it is a good second income."

Kashi's first income was as a successful hairstylist in New York City.

"No, I didn't know." I looked down at the rows of gemmed accessories and stifled a shiver. There had to be hundreds of Kashi's sparkly cockroach-like pins with swirls of different colored hair swooping out from the sides.

He narrowed his eyes. "Where is *your* special Kashi 'Get Out of Town Titanic'?"

Kashi named all his brooches and had given me one at the end of the cruise. "The brooch with a black spider and sinking ship?"

He smiled, remembering it fondly. "That is the one."

"Uh, I must've left it at home." Yeah, pinned to my pest-control cupboard of Raid and Black Flag.

"I bet you get a lot of compliments when you wear it."

"You have no idea."

"Yes, I do have some idea. Where else can you find such matchless beauty?"

I gazed down at the brooches, at a loss for words. "Nowhere."

"I've been busy, nonstop, topping my old creations." He bounced along the length of his table and held up brooch after brooch. "There's my 'Get Out of Town Sushi,' 'Get Out of Town JLo,' 'Get Out of Town Mr. Darcy'…for romance lovers, and even my 'Get Out of Town Fräulein' for…well, it is to be determined who it is for as I have not sold any yet."

Ha. "Does it have a witch's hat and cauldron?"

"No." He looked confused, no idea I was thinking of Candace. "But I take special orders."

"I'll keep that in mind."

"I do the odd craft show and festival." He waved his sleeved arm around the tent like it was his castle. "Since there was an opening for a spot here, I flew in from New York and contracted a shingle."

I suppressed a grin. As usual, Kashi mixed up his sayings. "You mean you hung out your shingle. In other words, you started selling your brooches here."

"Indeed. That is what I said."

I motioned over my shoulder to the other tent. "Do you know Pandi Gupta?"

Kashi tidied his brooches. "Of course. I know Pandi very well. We belong to the same sports club. Just because I am in New York does not mean I am man on the moon."

Indubitably. Man on Mars, maybe.

He chuckled. "Pandi is a business genius. He could sell sand to an Eskimo."

"You mean ice."

"Why would an Eskimo want ice?"

Oh brother.

His eyes popped out. "But do be careful when you speak to him. Pandi is scared of insects. He has a phobia, I believe. Will scream like a chicken if a bug comes near." He thought for a moment. "Good thing you did not wear your 'Get Out of Town Titanic' today. The spider might've given Pandi a cardiac arrest."

"Yes, I noticed he dislikes flies."

"Dislikes! That is to put it mildly."

I gave Kashi a calculating look. How much did he know about today's incident? I leaned across the table more aggressively than I meant to. "Did you hear his business partner Woody MacDunnell was discovered murdered in the park?"

"Aah!" he yelped, hands up, a fearful look in his eyes. "No, I did not." He backed away from me. "Does this mean you will attack me again with a sword? I swear I did not kill any Woody MacDunnell."

I smiled, recalling our sword fight on the cruise ship. "Relax. I'm not attacking anyone. And that sword was foam, remember?"

"I remember you kicked my scrawny brown butt."

The smile widened inside. I did know how to kick butt, especially when I was forced into it. "I'm merely asking questions. Finding out what people knew about Woody."

"Count me out. I know nothing."

After a bit of coaxing, he promised to keep his ear to the floor—or ground, as it were. Then he got busy showing his brooches to a group of people who entered the tent.

I said *so long* and stepped outside, hoping Max would materialize. I searched left and right and up and down the row of booths. No Max. Hmm. What was he up to? And why was I looking for more trouble? Well, I wasn't one to stand around and wait for something to happen.

Mentally, I rewound to my conversation in Pandi's tent with the woman admiring mood rings. She appeared to know a thing or two about them and what the colors signified. Then it hit me. Twix! I had to call her. See what she could offer.

I dug my phone out of my bag and rang her up.

"What is it this time?" she asked. "Code Romero or code de Marco?"

If Max won first place for being the wisenheimer in my life, Twix ran a close second. I glared at the phone, then put it back to my ear. "What's that supposed to mean?"

The kids were yelling in the background, and it sounded like a heap of toy blocks crashed to the floor. "It means the only time you call lately is when you're in trouble with one of the hunky men in your life." She sighed as if she could scarcely imagine such an existence when the truth was, Twix married a hunk right out of high school. True, Tony worked on feet all day as a podiatrist for the Red Sox. But it could've been worse. I wasn't sure what was worse than dealing with fungal infections, warts, and hammertoes, but there had to be something.

"Or you're involved in another mystery." Another dreamy sigh.

"How'd you guess?"

I filled her in on Woody's murder and what I knew so far. She muffled the phone, hollered at the kids to be quiet, then came back on the line. "Jeepers creepers. I wanted to get to the multicultural fair, but the kids are down with the flu. And Tony's deep in the Sox schedule and isn't home all weekend. So what's this about a mood ring?"

"Do you still have yours from high school? If I recall, you worshipped that thing."

"Darn tootin'. I could always count on it to tell me my moods. Not that I needed a ring for that, but it was kind of fun to see how accurate it was. What do you want to know?"

"What the colors mean. When I found it, it had just left Woody's finger. It went from turquoise to purple."

"Turquoise to purple, huh? It's been a while, but I believe those colors mean cool, subdued."

"Splendid. Couldn't get more subdued than dead."

"See? Told you it was accurate."

"What about when it turns yellow?"

"Aha. Did you see Handsome? Get all hot and bothered by his presence? I take it Romero's back, working the case."

Sheesh. How much power did these rings have? "How about when it glows green?"

"Green signifies romance or, to a lesser extent, being relaxed. Who was wearing it at this point?"

I explained how Romero's mother ran into Woody during the festival setup and how she saw the green glow on his ring.

"Was he romantically involved with someone at the fair?" Twix wanted to know.

"Up until now, I wasn't sure." I pictured the mood rings under glass in the Indian tent and Adia's face when I broke the news that Woody had been killed. Something had niggled me about her reaction, but was it a leap to wonder if she'd been dating him? Had she given him the ring? Did they have a rendezvous before the coffee break?

"But you're sure *now*." Twix broke into my thoughts. "Rats. I miss all the fun."

"I don't know. One last question. What does red signify?" I had an inkling I knew the answer to this.

"Ooh. Red means aggression or fear."

Bingo. The color Tantig saw at the porta potty. Woody was clearly embroiled in some type of squabble when she happened along. Was he arguing with Malton? Whoever it was, the person had to have hidden as Tantig hobbled up.

I thanked Twix for the help and vowed I'd be in touch soon.

"Yeah, sure," she said before ringing off. "Next time we clean the shop, you better bring chocolate. And booze," she added, chuckling.

Cleaning the salon was our weekly to biweekly date with each other. Twix helped me scour the place, and I turned her into a beauty queen for a day. I made a mental note to add chocolate and wine to our next cleaning spree, then hung up.

I backtracked into the second tent, hoping to find Max and Adia. I was in luck. They were talking and laughing at the counter, and Adia was back to folding blouses.

A customer approached Adia and asked for help. Adia led the woman to a clothing rack, giving Max a demure smile as she strode by. Max seemed to heighten an inch in his shoes. He turned, all aglow, then noticed me, and wandered over.

"Where'd *you* go, Prince Charming?" I teased.

He attempted to act carefree and aimed his thumb over his shoulder. "Adia was showing me something in the back room."

I poked my head past him. "There's another room?"

"It's for staff. I asked Adia about the elephant statues, and she said there were more in the back."

I gazed at the various-sized bronze and wooden elephants taking up a small corner of the tent. I leaned on one leg, playfulness spilling out of my voice. "Now you're interested in elephant statues?" It was always something with Max.

He turned and watched Adia with a lingering smile, then reluctantly swiveled back and studied me. "Maybe."

I treaded carefully. "Anything else you're interested in?"

He shushed me and groaned out a sigh. "Okay. Is it that obvious I find her attractive?"

I faked a frown. "Not in the least. I stare at everyone with my mouth hanging to my knees and my heart bursting through my shirt."

He cocked his head at me. "Funny, I thought that look was reserved for Romero. Or wait. Was it for Jock?"

"Smartass." Watching Max fawn over a woman was odd, but maybe I'd had him all wrong. He'd never once stated his sexual preference, and I'd never pried into his personal life. Come to think of it, he *oohed* and *ahhed* at women as much as he did men. Max was a perfectionist and loved anything of beauty. Chalk Adia up as a thing of beauty.

His eyes brightened. "Anyway, you've got it all wrong. We hit it off right away at camp during those two weeks. She appeared different than anyone I'd ever met, and we became fast friends. Then we lost touch. I think they moved around a lot, and I don't believe I ever knew her last name. I sure didn't recognize it. But I thought her dad was an accountant. Things must've changed." He shrugged. "Now that she's here, we're getting to know each other again. No harm in that, right?"

"Right." I guess. "Does this mean you no longer want to help me with the case?"

"No. We're buddies till the end. I would never desert you."

Yeah, I'd heard that before.

He made a face at my cynical look. "*Okay*. I almost left you to work for Candace. That was before I realized she was a rotting piece of fungus with a bond to Satan and the burning underworld."

I grinned. "Tell me how you really feel."

He eyed me squarely. "But there's got to be more to this desire of yours to catch a killer than purely wanting to find out who murdered Woody. And though Candace has upped the stakes, I can see it in your face there's something else. What gives? What aren't you telling me?"

I stared at him for a fraction of a second, shifted my gaze to Adia, then focused on the ground, my heart suddenly so heavy, it felt like it had dropped to my feet.

"What is it, Kemosabe?" Max lifted my chin, his voice soft. He blinked at the tears in my eyes but had the good grace not to mention them. Unlike his usual self, he waited patiently for me to divulge.

"*Tell* me!" His eyes watered. He wiped his tears, then reached over and squeezed my lashes. "You're going to ruin what I just fixed."

I sniffed and straightened my back. "If you laugh, I'll never forgive you."

"I promise." He made the sign of the cross over his chest in good faith.

"It's the park."

"What park?"

"*This* park."

He dragged me outside the tent, then looked around like he was missing something. "I don't get it."

"How could you? You didn't have the same experiences I had growing up."

"You mean the bullying and teasing?"

"Yes." Max knew about the cruel pranks the popular girls at school had played on me. But I'd never told him I used to escape to Rueland Town Park. "When the bullying got unbearable, I'd ride my bike here. It was the only place I felt safe." I drew on the memories like it was yesterday. "I found solace feeding the ducks, walking the footbridges, or sitting in the gazebo beneath the flickering lights. I could cry without hiding my tears or feeling shame. Since I was practically invisible, no one ever bothered me here."

Max wiped his eyes again, then did a full three-sixty, ogling the park with new lenses. He stopped face to face and looked down at me. "I get it now. This park means a lot to you. We have to find the murderer and give this site its rightful place in society...a place where others can come to find themselves and feel safe."

I swiped the back of my hand across my nose. "Thanks, Max, for understanding."

He gave me a brief hug. "That's what big brothers are for."

I grinned. If Max had been a brother, I would've pounded him a hundred times by now. Nonetheless, at moments like this, I appreciated his concern.

"One request..." He turned halfway toward the tent. "You mind if I take the odd break to check in on Adia? Like now?"

My eyebrows shot up to my hairline. "You just left her

two minutes ago. What do you need to check? If she sneezed while you were gone?"

He flattened his lips, not amused at my wit. "She was disturbed when she learned Woody had been murdered." He shook his head. "Must be hard when her dad and Woody had been so close."

Yes. Hard. The cynic in me jumped to all kinds of notions. Like could there have been more to Adia's reaction about Woody's death than merely worrying about her father? For Max's sake, I kept my mouth shut.

"I swear, I won't be gone long, and if I am, I'll let you know."

I scrounged around in my bag and finally whipped out my phone. "I'll be ready, my phone at the helm."

"Great. If *that's* what we're depending on, we're in trouble." He rolled his eyes and grabbed my phone. "Have you even charged this thing since last week?"

Technology and I didn't get along. Automatically, I surveyed the park, not paying much attention to Max fiddling with my device.

"Look." He pointed to the top right corner of my screen. "Eighteen percent means the battery is low."

I snatched my phone away from him. "I'm aware of that. I wasn't born yesterday. I'll charge it when I get home."

"Marvelous. And when I need you, your phone will be dead."

"If you're with Adia, you won't need me." I winked and dumped my phone back in my bag.

"True." He put on a cheery face and wheeled around to the tent. "Back in a jiffy."

Chapter 8

Next on my list was a talk with Hoagy MacEwen. Though I'd filled Max in on my chat with Barn, I hadn't elaborated on MacEwen or MacGregor.

I wasn't sure what to make of Hoagy's ornery disposition, but I was convinced he knew something about Woody's death. Deep down, gut instinct told me Malton was also wrapped up in this. Maybe it was the glower Hoagy had given him at their booth earlier. Or was it Malton's criminal record that triggered these thoughts? Or his argument with Woody that Aileen had witnessed? The nagging persisted that these gentlemen were hiding something. Though language was a barrier with Hoagy, I was going to find a way to communicate if it was the last thing I did.

Max agreed we should talk to both men, then got distracted by the smell of cotton candy and the inviting candy booth in front of us. Since my stomach had settled and Max wouldn't stop nattering about buying the sweet fluff, we stopped for an extra-large bag.

We separated fibers of pink and blue candy floss like yarn, and instantly Kashi's spindly hair brooches came to mind.

While Max stuffed his face, I told him about my visit with Kashi, sharing how he and Pandi belonged to the same sports club. "Apart from sword-fighting," I mused, "who knew Kashi was into sports?"

Max shrugged. "He seems fit."

"That he does." I bit my lip. "I think he peed his pants when I told him about the slaying in the park."

Max held the plastic bag open for me. "Can you blame him for being scared? You all but hunted him down for murder on the cruise."

I gave him a deadpan stare. "If I remember correctly, *you* were the one pointing fingers at Kashi. And I quote, 'Kashi's our man. He looks all cheerful and up-and-up, but there's malice in those eyes.'" I tapped my toe on the ground. "Ring any bells, Sherlock?"

He blew out a sigh. "That was before he rid me of my anxiety over deep water. It takes a special person to care about others like that."

My face relaxed into a grin. "Yeah. Kashi *is* special."

"He *is*!" Doubting my sincerity, Max pulled the bag away from me.

I reached around his back for the cotton candy when we heard a death-shattering scream so loud that the mirror outside the tent beside us shattered to the ground.

Max and I gaped at each other, eyes wide. "Candace!" we said in unison.

We took off at high speed toward the pond, Kashi and his heroic deeds forgotten.

We froze twenty feet from the crime scene and witnessed Candace in her Bavarian dress slog out of the water, soaked and covered in seaweed, her over-the-knee stockings down by her ankles. Two of the dive team, escorting her out, pitched her heels on the ground. The uniforms on land had their arms folded in front, heads shaking, grins masked. That didn't stop Candace from trudging up to them, spitting in fury.

The classy thing to do would've been to flee and give Candace space to gain her self-respect. Unfortunately, being classy was overrated. We inched closer, watching the action unfold.

"If you think for one minute," Candace sputtered, fist shaking at Cop #1, "that a little water's going to keep me from finding Woody's murderer…then you've got another thing coming."

Cop #2 put his hand to his mouth and snickered behind his palm.

"That goes for you, too!" Candace swiped a glob of seaweed from her chest and flung it at their feet.

She stomped two feet past the cops and came to a sudden halt, alarm carved on her face, her pallor, white. Something had the power to flummox Candace, and we swiveled to see what it was.

I gasped in surprise at the man striding up to her, and Max uttered, "Huh?"

"That's Hoagy MacEwen," I whispered.

He stopped in front of Candace and wasted no time shouting at her in his thick Scottish brogue.

Why was Hoagy here and not at his booth? And why was he yelling at Candace?

"What are you waiting for?" Max tore off another piece of cotton candy. "You wanted to talk to him."

"Very funny." I went to backhand him in the gut, but Max had gotten quicker, leaping out of the way.

"Sounds like a lovers' quarrel," he said, finishing his bite.

I looked at him like the cotton candy wasn't the only thing light and fluffy. "What are you yakking about? Candace just met Hoagy today."

We gawked at each other at that. It wasn't a secret that Candace moved fast when it came to men. The *Rueland News* could do a two-page spread on the woman's romantic exploits.

We leaned in, trying to decipher what Hoagy was saying, but his words were like gibberish. I doubted Candace knew what he said either. Hoagy sighed in exasperation, muttered something under his breath, then threw her over his back like a sack of haggis, and stamped away.

"That settles that." Max squashed the empty bag and chucked it in a nearby trash bin.

"What's that supposed to mean?" I followed his footsteps, still in shock over Hoagy hauling off Candace.

"It *means*, my dear naïve friend, that Hoagy is taking Miss Bavaria back to his cave where he shall pound her with his instrument. And I don't mean the bagpipes."

I made a face at his illustration. "Please. My stomach just settled. I don't need bad visuals of Hoagy porking Candace." I gave him a second glance, reassessing his words. "What makes you think the guy's even interested in our *fräulein*? You saw him shouting at her."

"True. Barbarian is simply the language some men speak. The angrier the voice, the more taken they are with their mate." He targeted me. "I do believe you've experienced this phenomenon with Mr. Long Arm of the Law. Also known as hot, sexy Detective Romero."

I waved Max away, not willing to admit I'd been turned on by the shouting matches I'd had with Romero. But the flutter in my groin proved Max was onto something.

"And if you want to talk to Mr. MacEwen," he concluded, "it's going to be through Candace." He did a one-shoulder shrug. "Face it, lovey. She's got the upper hand…here anyway."

"Terrific. I'd rather talk to Malton MacGregor, a known convict with arrogance up the ying-yang."

Max smiled brightly. "Then what are we waiting for?"

We wandered the grounds with no luck finding MacGregor. That was okay with me. I wasn't in a rush to talk to him. Probably due to the vibe that screamed *stay away*.

Max had gone a whole hour without seeing Adia and chose this moment to ask if he could check on her.

"She's taking a break," he said, reading off his phone. "Said she'd meet up with me by the Ferris wheel."

I restrained from rolling my eyes. "Go. Knock yourself out."

"You sure?"

No, I wasn't sure. About any of this. The murder. Pandi. Hoagy. Adia. Max reuniting with Adia—a woman he barely remembered, a woman I suspected knew more about Woody's demise than she was letting on. But in the immortal words of my right-hand man, I had to face facts.

"Yes, I'm sure."

Max was a highly intelligent individual. He'd take his time getting to know Adia again. If there was anything that seemed off, he'd be the first to see it. That, of course, depended on whether he could get past her beauty and those hypnotic green eyes. Oh Lord. I was in trouble.

Max took off with a happy trot, and I stood there, thinking about my next move. I certainly wasn't going to wait around for Lover Boy to ride the Ferris wheel into the sunset with Miss India. It was past suppertime, night was closing in, and I had things to do.

Since Malton was nowhere in sight, I'd concentrate on Pandi. What better way than to sneak into that back room of his tent and see if there were any clues that could point to a soured partnership with Woody. Pandi wanted me to believe their relationship was rosy, but nothing was ever as it seemed. We had two different people from two diverse backgrounds. That in itself provided opportunity for conflict.

If my thinking was on track, the back room would be set up like a temporary office. Sure, it housed extra merchandise like revered elephant statues, but if Pandi was as successful as I kept hearing, I was betting he ran his business while managing the tent. With luck, I might find something important scattered about.

Only problem with this idea was Pandi. What if he was in the back room? I'd never get access. I argued that if Adia was off having her fun with Max, then Pandi would be out front running the tent. In that case, it'd be safe to creep in through the back.

I bypassed the main thoroughfare and hightailed it to the rear alley. Vendors' vehicles and the odd Dumpster lined a curb behind each country's tent. A vendor flipped back the door flap to his tent, walked to his truck, and grabbed supplies. He gave me a strange look, then darted back inside.

Not sure what the look was about, I paused at my reflection in the full-length mirror resting against the side of a van. Yep. Spiked heels. Snug dress. Sparkly earrings. And don't forget…false eyelashes. I fluttered the silly things, which were hanging on by a thread. *Ugh*. If I'd been dressed in my ethnic garb, the guy wouldn't have looked twice.

What if someone asked questions? Why was I back here? What tent was I working? No one would believe I was helping at the Armenian booth, dressed like this. Better to have a plan in place. I had no idea what that plan was, but my nerves were a jumbled mess, and perspiration was seeping out my pores. I had to think of something quick.

The van's sliding doors were open, and Asian conical paddy hats were piled high inside. I knew better than to pinch one, but I had no choice. I nabbed a hat off the backseat and plopped it on my head. What could it hurt?

With my rice hat low over my face, I skipped past door flap after door flap, remembering the order of tents by country as I passed. Aha! India! Complete with curry smell and sitar music.

Pushing back my hat so I could see, I skirted past the food tent and found the entrance to Pandi's back room. I peeked through the flap, and in a quiet shaky tone, called his name.

No response. Just music and the hum of voices in the distance.

Taking this as a sign of encouragement, I slipped inside and let my eyes adjust to the large area. *Okay, Miss Marple. Now what?* Other than stacks of merchandise piled five feet high and rows of elephant statues on the floor, there wasn't a whole lot to root through.

I edged past items lining both walls and spotted a table and chair in the far corner. It was nothing more than a card table, but I was pleased to see it.

I dashed over, hastily taking in file folders, pens, notepads, used coffee cups, and plastic containers of Indian-food leftovers.

Shoving my hat out of the way, I rifled through the folders, coming across blueprints and other plans labeled Gupta's Getaways. That was all well and good, but I didn't need to know structural data or what designs were going into the building. I already saw that it looked like the Taj Mahal. What I needed was something on a personal note. Something that proved dissension between Pandi and Woody.

Wait. What was this?

Tucked under the file folders were half a dozen unfinished memos addressed to Woody. *I need to know where things stand,* read one. *This is the last time I'm asking,* read another. Each note conveyed similar messages with little else. Like the person was trying to find the right words to finish his or her thoughts.

A tremor slid up my neck. Who'd been writing notes to Woody? And why? Was it Adia? Pandi? Were they hints of unrequited love, or threats of some kind? I couldn't judge anything from the handwriting since it was average in appearance. Not especially neat, like one would expect from a woman, and not scratchy like that of most men.

Unless I witnessed something written by the father-daughter team, the only thing I could do was filch one of the notes and show Romero. He'd find out who the penman was. Of course, he wouldn't be too thrilled with my snooping. But that wouldn't be a first.

By accident, my knee bumped something beside the table. I tilted my head down and spotted a wastepaper basket one-third full of crumpled notepaper. Pushing my nuisance of a hat back again, I crouched in front of the basket and unfolded several pieces of paper. More of the same messages. No clue as to who wrote them.

I was about to stuff a note in my bag when my hat flopped down yet again. *Oof.* There was no winning. Out of frustration, I whipped off the bothersome thing, nicking loose my false lashes from my outer left lid in the process. *Enough of this.* I tore off the lashes at the same time a loud *slap* sounded on the table by my ear. Then a pair of bony hands wrapped around my neck.

I yelped and reflexively flung my lashes over my shoulder while wrestling to loosen my assailant's chokehold.

"*Eeeee!*" The maniac raised his hands from squeezing the life out of me, screeching like there was a four-alarm fire.

Heart thumping, pulse racing, I spun around and faced Pandi who'd fallen ass-backward to the ground. "Are you *crazy?*" I scrambled to my feet, rubbing my neck, swiping his stupid fly swatter to the ground beside him.

"*Me* crazy!" He clasped his fly swatter and sprang to his feet. "You are in no position to call *me* crazy. And where is that spider?" He flung boxes left and right. "I saw it a second ago. *Aah!*" he shrieked, hoisting a wooden elephant in the air. "Did it crawl under that box?"

I ducked before the flying elephant hit me in the head. "It wasn't a spider."

He tossed more cartons in the air. "I know a spider when I *see* one." He dropped his fly swatter, lunged for the table, and peeked underneath. "Where did it go?" He jiggled the table, then took his arm and cleared everything from it.

Plastic food containers, file folders, and coffee cups flew to the ground.

"*Relax!*" I cried. "You're ruining the place."

He hopped from foot to foot. "If I do not find that spider, this whole *tent* will be ruined."

Oy vey. This guy may have been a business genius, but he was loony tunes in the real-life department. I ripped off my other false eyelash, glad to be free of the damn things. "*This* is what you saw."

He looked up at me twirling the black lashes between my fingers. "*Aaaaah!*" He crashed to the floor again and crab-walked away from me.

"They're only false eyelashes." I leaned over him, arms out, displaying what I'd removed. "I tore one off and accidentally threw it at you."

Just then, Kashi rushed into the room. "Pandi! Are you o—" He cut his words short and gaped from Pandi, frozen mid crab-walk, to me, arms stretched over him. There was a moment's pause, Kashi's mind taking it all in, then he swiveled on his heels and took off.

Pandi sighed, hand to chest, calming himself. "You are absolutely certain it was not a spider. My heart would not take it."

"Positive." I stowed the lashes in my bag and helped him to his feet.

"Then for the big question, Miss Valentine. What are you doing in my tent? This room is for employees only."

This was the part I dreaded. "Uh…" I looked around the wrecked room for inspiration. "I was searching for a particular elephant statue. *This* one!" I kicked a box out of my way and rushed over to the statue he'd just tossed. It was big and unwieldly with a fuchsia gem stuck to its forehead.

He brightened. "Why didn't you say so? We keep these back here for serious buyers."

"That's me. A serious buyer." I put on a big smile and stroked the elephant's tusks as if it were a trophy. "How much?"

"Since you are a celebrated woman in this town, I give it to you for a good price. Two hundred and eighty dollars."

"Two-eighty!" I choked. "How much if I wasn't celebrated?"

"Two hundred and eighty-two." He beamed like it was the deal of the century.

"Gee, thanks." I tried to add gratitude behind the smile, but I was unsuccessful.

He picked up the three-foot-high statue and snagged the price tag. "Do you want it wrapped?"

"No." I paid him, thinking of the shoes I could've bought with this money. "I'll carry it like this. Thanks."

He held open the tent flap and ushered me out. "Wait." He turned around, rushed back into the room, and produced my rice hat. "Do not forget this."

I plunked the hat on my head, and like the idiot I was, thanked him and said farewell. *Drat.* Not only was I hauling a costly twenty-pound behemoth under my arm, but I missed my chance to pocket one of the messages to show Romero. *Dumb, Valentine. Dumb.*

I might've messed up here, but I was going to get sharper. What that looked like, I didn't know.

Chapter 9

Shielding my eyes from the setting sun, I scurried over to the paddy-hat van and tossed my ill-gotten gain back inside. "Thanks for nothing," I said under my breath, not sure if I was more upset with the hat or my stupidity. I gawked down at my wooden elephant and its morose eyes, the answer to that, obvious.

I stood there, deciding what to do with my new purchase, when it was ripped from my arms and thrown to the ground. Before I could react, Malton MacGregor drifted in front of me and backed me several feet behind the van.

"You think you're hot stuff, don't you?" He had no accent whatsoever, but he reeked of smoker's breath, using this opportunity to pull out a fresh cigarette.

My heart was in my throat, and my mouth was suddenly dry. "If you don't back off," I said more boldly than I felt, "I'm going to scream."

He smirked, the face of a handsome man who often got his way. "I wouldn't do that if I were you." He lit his cigarette in a slow, methodical manner and held the scorched end an inch from my face. A friendly warning to keep quiet.

He studied my eyes and lips, smiling in crude assessment. Then he took a deep drag.

"What do you want?" I asked, not daring to move.

He exhaled smoke up into the air, laughing as if we were old friends. "If I told you what I wanted, you'd probably slap my face."

I rounded my hands into fists. I'd love to slap his face even if he *didn't* tell me what he wanted.

"But to keep it clean, let me give you a piece of advice. Stop snooping into Woody's death. He died, and it's unfortunate. But nothing's going to bring him back."

"You say that as if you're glad he's gone."

He raised an eyebrow but didn't give anything away. That didn't deter me from riling him more. "What happened? You owe him money you couldn't pay? He threaten to go to the police? Not so good when you've got a criminal record."

His eyes flashed with fury, but he kept himself in check, not letting me get under his skin.

He flicked his cigarette to the ground, twirled me around in his arms, and banged me against his chest, his breath at my ear, his palm edging my breast. "You seem to know a lot about me, love. No fun in that. Better to take things nice and slow." At that, he took his thumb and stroked my neck.

Rage boiled to the surface to the point that I was seeing double. On instinct, I bit down hard on his hand.

"*Ah.* You *bitch.*" He pulled my hair and yanked my head back. "You're going to pay for that."

Out of nowhere, there was a shift in the air, and I felt Malton stiffen. The familiar scent of Arctic Spruce drifted my way along with a deep, confident voice I'd come to trust. "Take your hands off the lady. *Now.*" His tone was lethal, his words, clipped. The tingles surging through my body verified it. Romero was the force behind the threat.

Malton loosened his hold on me, not tempting the authority in Romero's voice. I bounced forward and whirled around. Exhaling, I ran to pick up my elephant, then waited to see who made the next move.

Romero twisted Malton's arm high behind his back, using his strength to intimidate the guy.

Malton got the hint and sneered in pain. "We were just having a friendly chat."

"Didn't look that way to me." Romero tightened his grip, and at once a mix of pride for his valor and fear for what he might do raced through my blood. "If I see you anywhere near Valentine again, I'll make you sorry you ever laid eyes on her." He curled Malton's arm higher and slammed him against the van, slanting close to his ear. "Got that, *friend*?" Without waiting for a response, he yanked him back and shoved him five feet in the opposite direction. "Go back to that rock you crawled out from."

Malton wiped a string of drool from his mouth and scowled at Romero. Wisely, he kept from speaking. He straightened his collar, ran his hand through his hair, and shuffled away.

I let out a pent-up breath and cuddled close to my elephant. My hands were trembling, and my chest, aching. I tried to calm myself, but I kept picturing what would've happened if Romero hadn't come along. My bag was by my side, but I was so startled by my aggressor, I didn't think to reach into it for a defense.

I recalled Max's nervous sigh, the one that said maybe this time my bag wouldn't provide safety when I needed it. I told myself I was simply taken by surprise. That was all.

Romero zeroed in on me with the look of a man who'd just done battle, and something told me our exchange wasn't going to go well. "Listen to me…"

I didn't care to listen. I dropped my bag and elephant to the ground, ran up to him, and threw my arms around his neck. I kissed his tightly drawn lips with the passion of a woman completely enamored with her hero. It was out of character, and the timing wasn't great, but I didn't care. He felt so good and made me feel like I was everything in the world to him.

Despite that self-assured feeling that had returned, an alarming thought struck me. Romero was a man who took control, who commanded others. *He* was the one who made the advances. But he didn't reject me or the kiss, regardless of my timing. His full lips yielded, and he wrapped his arms around me, molding me into his aroused form. He roved his hands up and down my dress like a man who knew how to handle a woman's body, a man who liked confidence in a woman.

What seemed like hours later, we broke apart, eyes locked on each other. My heart was pounding, my lips numb, and my insides fluttered with butterflies.

He wiped his mouth with the back of his wrist and gave me a second to catch my breath. Then he drew me in again. In a gentle manner, he pressed his lips on my forehead. "You okay?"

I dared to grin up into his probing eyes. "You're asking me that *now*?" I nestled into his arms, accepting his warmth and strength, inhaling his wonderful smell. "I'm fine. Thank you."

"It's me who should be thanking *you*." He pulled us apart, his look turning primal, like he wanted to devour me with another hot kiss. "You know I'm a patient man but, lass, I'm running out of patience."

I knew what he was referring to, and I couldn't blame him. We'd been dating for months, and between his work schedule and my fear of commitment, we hadn't taken things to the next level. Not willing to address the issue, I skipped around it. "Since when did you start uttering Scottish terms?"

The virile look intensified, the danger element coming out like it always did at erotic moments. "Since I started undressing you with my eyes."

"You did that *before* you used the term *lass*." I stared into his gorgeous face, the coarse scar on his cheekbone pulling me in.

Okay, I reasoned, Romero had told me he loved me...in so many words. He'd written it with a tube of hand cream and served it in a roomful of people. But the sentiment was the same.

Our time apart had escalated the sexual tension between us at death-breaking speed. But I wasn't one to be forced into anything. Maybe I took longer than the average person to share myself intimately. But I'd jumped in with both feet before, and look how that had turned out. I was a vulnerable mess with trust issues. I admitted it. Logic told me I couldn't keep doing the same things expecting different results. This time I wanted to be sure.

I worked at calming the stirring inside because there was no fooling: I wanted Romero *bad*. Maybe a dinner date…or something special when this case was over. I'd have time then to reassess how I felt.

Romero strode over to the elephant, picked it off the ground, and lifted an eyebrow at me. "Yours?"

I flashed back to my episode with Pandi, calculating what to say next. What the hell. I'd been in trouble before. If I could provide insight into the case, it'd be worth it. I shared what I'd done earlier, told Romero about Pandi's business, the mood rings on display in his tent, and the written notes I'd uncovered.

"Uh-huh." He rolled his tongue around in his mouth.

"Is that it?" I raised my voice sweetly, hoping it'd keep him calm.

"For now." He shook his head. "I've got too much on my plate to lecture you."

I could live with that.

"Just so you know," he continued, "I'm aware of Pandi's partnership with Woody. We're following up on a few leads." He paused. "Not sure where you're going with the mood rings or the notes, but I trust you have a theory."

"I have a theory, all right." I stabbed my hands on my hips, ignoring his flippant tone. "Adia could've been involved with Woody, given him the ring, and even scribbled those notes."

"Hold on. Adia?"

"Pandi's daughter. An Indian version of Princess Jasmine."

"The Disney princess." He rocked on his heels, hiding what he thought of the comparison.

"*Yes*." I widened my eyes, my idea evolving, though I hated thinking such thoughts about someone Max had once known. "Maybe she killed Woody. You know, a woman scorned."

He scooped my bag off the ground and handed it to me, probably to keep from losing his composure. "And she'd be a woman scorned *because*?"

"Because Woody was a ladies' man. What if they'd been dating, and he was playing the field?" I swung my bag over my shoulder. "What if Adia found out and started giving him ultimatums? Hence, the notes. Let's say Woody didn't care, said he wasn't going to stop his pursuits. What if she flew into a jealous rage and murdered him?"

"That's a lot of what ifs. And so far, Nancy Drew, you haven't given me any indication how you knew they were dating."

I snatched the elephant from him, wanting to whack it on his wise-guy head. "Woman's intuition. I can't explain, but she gave a look when I mentioned Woody's murder."

"What kind of look?"

"I don't know. A look that said she knew more than she was letting on."

He blew out a sigh, tired of going around in circles. "I'll leave that with you."

I gasped. "You're dismissing this?"

He peered down the alley, waited while a vendor retrieved something from his truck, then centered on me like he couldn't believe he was having a serious conversation with a woman clutching a half-ton elephant. "Look, you may be onto something. And there's a chance a woman knocked off Woody. But it's not likely."

"Why not? Granted, Adia is tiny, but Woody wasn't a big man. If she came up from behind him silently, she could've thunked him on the head with the canoe paddle."

He assumed the cop stance, his expression grave. "Nobody *said* it was a canoe paddle."

"*You* did."

His words were measured, a sure sign Romero was losing his temper. "To be exact, *you* suggested the murder weapon was a canoe paddle. All *I* said was it was possible."

He had me there. "Have you found any other murder weapon?"

"The search continues."

"Then it's possible it *was* a canoe paddle."

A groan fled his lips. "Yes, it's possible. If you see someone walking around with one, let me know."

I narrowed my eyes to slits, not liking his cocky humor one bit. "You still haven't said why it's not likely Adia was the murderer."

Scrubbing his chin was a tactic I'd seen Romero perform in the past. Of course, it was always done in fits of frustration, like now. "Do you ever give up?"

I blinked up at him, waiting a beat before answering. "No."

He sought the darkening sky in wordless prayer, then lowered his chin and moved in, cool, calm, and collected. "We're looking at other leads. Satisfied?"

"Yeah, you said that already. And not nearly."

"What I *didn't* say was you should go home before it's totally dark and the park closes."

I gave him an indignant stare. "Just so you know, I was *planning* on going home." I wasn't offering that I was returning after dark to do some digging. Certain things were better left unsaid.

"Good. And take that oversized Heidi with you. Bad enough I've got one persistent hairstylist meddling in things. I don't need a second."

By the sound of it, Romero hadn't had the pleasure of meeting Candace...until today. If he thought I was going to persuade her to do anything, he was sorely mistaken. I had plenty of difficulties keeping track of my own affairs. I had no intention of tackling Candace.

"Sorry, bub." I secured my hold on my elephant...Ellie. Yes. Ellie. A fondness for the bulky thing had grown on me. "You're on your own with that one."

I took one last look at him in his denim shirt and perfectly filled-out jeans, then turned in a huff and stomped off with Ellie's butt swinging behind me.

Before I left the park, I detoured to my parents' booth to see how Tantig's hand was and ask if there was anything I could do before I went home.

My mother sent off a couple with two kebab combos and a stack of napkins, then thrust a skewer in my face. "Here. Eat."

The smell of barbequed seasoned beef made my mouth water. "I'm fine," I insisted.

"*Fine?* What did you eat today? Apart from your usual breakfast of Cocoa Puffs."

I smiled innocently. "I actually had Honeycombs this morning."

"Dear God. Then what have you eaten since you got to the park?"

"Pink cotton candy." I mustered an assertive voice. "Then I had blue cotton candy."

She smacked the skewer on the counter. "*Cotton candy*. That's nothing but sugar."

"Not true. There's also food coloring. And don't forget the flavoring."

A lecture was coming, but it felt good to release some tension, even if it was in the form of arguing with my mother. To be honest, I would've loved nothing more than to sit down for a kebab platter. But I had things to do, and I didn't want to waste time eating when I needed to prepare for a night of slinking around the park.

"You're too thin." My mother eyed me resolutely over the counter. "You need fat on your bones, like Holly."

Holly Dennison was my older sister and a vice detective. She was fair while I was dark. She talked tough while I watched my *P*'s and *Q*'s. She was big-boned and far from fat. I was small-boned and petite. Rather than get into it further, I glimpsed at the pink sky.

"I have to go. I came by to see how Tantig is and ask if there's anything I can do before I head home."

"You go ahead." My mother popped a container of pilaf in their cooler, simultaneously assuring me Tantig was fine. This was a relief. Guilt, Armenian style, niggled me all day that her injury had been my fault. After all, I, Valentine Beaumont, had the ability to be everywhere at all times and should've known better than to neglect helping at their booth. That was what the guilt had implied. But I cut myself some slack. My great-aunt was sitting on a lawn chair in the corner of the canopy, eating shish kebab and tabbouleh, her bandaged hand long forgotten.

My mother narrowed in on me. "I'm glad you're going home instead of playing Charlie's Angels." She lowered her voice. "You do know that this Woody fellow was murdered."

I froze at the mention of the homicide. "Yes. I heard. And I'm sure the police are doing everything in their power to find the culprit."

Right when I thought the inquisition was over, my mother jerked her head at Ellie like she just noticed my haul. "Why are you dragging around an elephant with a pink gem on its forehead?"

I angled my head down at Ellie and her exotic gem.

"I won it." I hated to lie. But I wasn't up to admitting I'd spent a bunch of money on a piece of wood that was only going to collect dust. Besides, Ellie was now mine, and she'd fit right in with the eclectic look in my Cape Cod bungalow.

"Couldn't you win something normal?" she asked. "Like a stuffed teddy bear? I saw someone toting a tiny one with a plaid kilt and a tam on its head. And it was squeezing iddy-biddy bagpipes. It was the sweetest thing."

It did sound sweet, but the mention of kilts took me back again to this morning's events and my mission to return to the park later. None of which I chose to share with my mother. "Why don't you get Dad to win you a teddy with a kilt?"

She slanted her head to the canopy on my right, *you can't be serious* scored on her face. "Your father's too busy playing goodwill ambassador."

I turned slightly and spied my father hamming it up with the Asian vendors next to them. I went from being relieved about Tantig to cringing for the whole of humanity. The problem wasn't that my father was mingling with others. He was simply a loose cannon when it came to making conversation with people holding different beliefs.

Since I couldn't stand by and wait for my father to say the wrong thing to the wrong person, I turned my back, put Ellie down, and texted Max, stating I was leaving the park and going home. I may have decided to return after closing, but I wouldn't be snooping in a dress and high heels—no matter how fetching they were, I thought cutely.

"Where are you, Max?" I muttered at his silence. Yeah, forget I asked. I knew exactly where he was and with whom. I wasn't duping myself into thinking Max would leave Adia until the park closed. Possibly, not even then. And what he did after that was his own business.

Suppressing the unease surrounding my heart over Max's budding reunion, I texted a final goodnight. I waited a few seconds. No answer. And everyone teased *me* about not using *my* phone. That was okey-dokey with this girl. I ditched it back in my bag, told my mother I'd see them tomorrow, and headed to my yellow Daisy Bug with Ellie. She could ride shotgun.

Following one of the paths, I approached the gazebo decked with flowers, ribbons, and twinkling lights that outlined the entire structure. I stopped to admire the landmark, glowing amidst the setting sun, pride filling me to swelling proportions. Teary-eyed, I set Ellie down and sat on her back, dragging my hand across my wet cheek. Darn this park, flooding me with memories.

Stop it, Valentine. You survived those mean girls. You even survived those horrendous dates. I grimaced sadly. Yeah, and there were quite a few of those.

I stared at the lights, regretful tears blurring my vision, when sudden images of a hard-headed cop with a gorgeous body and sexy swagger came to mind. If I were candid, I'd admit those weren't the only things that attracted me to Romero. I couldn't overlook his innate goodness. His patience. His strength and integrity. Whoa. Here was a thought. Was I pushing him away as punishment? Because I wanted him to pay for my bruised past?

I straightened and sniffed back tears, putting things into perspective. How was Romero responsible for the bullying I'd endured as a kid? How was he even responsible for the bad decisions I'd made? Was it because he was Iron Man, and I'd somehow expected him to stop the abuse...even when he hadn't been present?

I gave my head a shake at my attempt to psychoanalyze myself. Here I thought Pandi was loony tunes. I was no better.

I struggled to take a normal breath, recognizing the truth for what it was. Obviously, none of my past had anything to do with Romero. I knew that in my head and soul. Romero was decent, honest, and wholesome …er, regardless of his macho, bad-boy reputation. Okay, he'd been an Italian Stallion. He chose *me*, despite the wait, didn't he? I'd never experienced that kind of devotion before. Who *wouldn't* be lucky to have him?

A warm wave spread through my body, and I felt sappy all over. I sprang to my feet and swooped Ellie into my arms. I had to talk to Romero.

Instantly, a little voice in my head cried *stop* before I went any further. Now wasn't the time to profess my love for an overworked detective in the middle of a grisly murder case. Especially when this homicide had added to his existing load. He'd made *that* clear from the start.

I smoothed Ellie's head and reined in my emotions. For once, I'd act maturely and *not* on impulse. I was a woman in control, not some reckless youth who threw caution to the wind.

I reiterated my earlier vow. A dinner date…or something special when this case was done. There'd be time then to tell him how I felt. I gave an affirmative nod at my decision and hiked toward the footbridge bordering the parking lot.

The area was quiet, unlike the main thoroughfare where merchants were making the most of their last hour for the night, selling perishables at a discount.

I hoisted Ellie higher under my arm, pondering where I'd set her at home, when an uneasy feeling filled my bones. I froze mid-step, unable to nail the basis of my fear, but my hammering heart told me it was real. I waited a beat, my senses on high alert, my eyes focused on the smallest movement. Nothing stirred in front of me…which left behind me.

Gut instinct and my pulse thundering in my ears said I was being followed. I strained to detect movement, but the soft ground made sounds of footsteps hard to identify.

I was being paranoid. Who'd be following me? Candace? Playing Velma from *Scooby-Doo*? Candace wasn't the type to pussyfoot around. That left one person on my radar, the one creep who'd threatened me, who'd been humiliated and put in his place by Romero. Malton MacGregor. What if he was on the prowl, evening the score from earlier?

My nose twitched, and every muscle in my body tensed, the thought of Malton coming after me too much to bear. I inhaled a shaky breath, expecting to whiff cigarette smoke. *Nope.* Only lingering smells from the park.

I tightened my grip on Ellie. If anyone tried to attack me, I'd crack them on the skull with her. Poor thing. She'd had a rough day.

On pins and needles, I braced myself, then whirled around, ready to strike. The only thing in sight was the big green and blue globe mascot, prancing toward me. It jumped back and spread its arms wide, big white gloves up in surrender.

"Whew!" Relief sent my voice sky-high. Probably scared the bejeebers out of the poor guy…or girl. Doing a job like the rest of us.

I relaxed my grip on Ellie and nodded at the mascot. It lowered its arms, did a short tap dance in its blue stuffed shoes, then gave me a slow, deliberate wave.

I didn't know what that was all about, but in the pit of my stomach I wished this clown would turn and back away. As if understanding my thoughts, it spun around, tripped over its feet, and skipped back to the fair.

That was weird. I stood rooted, tamping down the nervousness rattling inside. The globe was probably done parading around for the night and heading home like me. And here I'd scared it off. Ridiculous things. Always in your face. What I hated most was that I'd been afraid of a silly stuffed mascot.

It'd been a long day, and I wasn't thinking straight.

Why should I be scared of someone in a goofy getup? Furthermore, who did I even know who'd dress the part?

They were good questions. If only I had good answers.

Chapter 10

My episode with the globe had given me a case of the jitters. Heading home was looking more inviting by the minute. If I could just put everything that had happened today behind me. But there were things that wouldn't let go. Not only the obvious, like Woody's murder. But something that should've dissipated from my mind by now. Where I'd first heard Pandi's name. I'd learned a lot about the businessman, but this still puzzled me.

Forget about it. There were things in life that remained a mystery. And in the grand scheme of things, it didn't matter since I'd already made his acquaintance. However, there was a part of me that felt it *did* matter, and that it could impact the case. Since I'd racked my brain and still couldn't come up with a personal connection, perhaps there'd be a clue at work. I had to find out.

I took the short cut to Darling and bounced into the parking lot I shared with Friar Tuck's. Cruising past the well-lit bakery, I wheeled to the left behind our buildings, steered around the Dumpster, and cut the engine by the back door of Beaumont's.

I grabbed my bag, locked the car doors, and after whiffing daylong fried donut smells, I let myself into the salon. I flicked on the lights and bolted the glass door behind me, remembering Jock and the broom fiasco that occurred last time I forgot to lock it. An electric charge shot through me at my idiocy. I wasn't going to make *that* mistake twice.

Safely locked inside, I coughed back the smell of hairspray that swam in the air from earlier and dashed down the hall. Who knew where Jock was anyway? Disappearing after depositing Phyllis in the first-aid tent. One thing was guaranteed. If he showed up at the shop, he'd have to use his key. Plus, my ears would be perked.

I turned right into the spacious Mediterranean-styled salon, omitting my usual peep at the grapevines and twinkling lights above the mirrors of the four cutting stations. They were among my favorite features of the shop, adding to the rustic feel, but I didn't have time to *ooh* and *ahh* at fixtures. I scooted past the folding screen into the square-shaped dispensary—our supply room and hangout between customers—then rolled the stool away and got right to the appointment book.

I flipped through the pages, picturing Pandi's neat, black hair. What if he'd been a client? Dozens of people came and went in a day—thanks to Jock being in my employment. I may not have seen every person who entered the shop, but surely I would've remembered whose hair I cut and recognized the name if it had been written down. But I was drawing a blank.

Going by Pandi's clean trim, I skimmed back two weeks. Any more time than that and his cut would've shown signs of age around the neck and ears. On the subject of cutting around the neck and ears, I eliminated Phyllis as the stylist…for obvious reasons.

But wait.

What if I'd been doing a facial or another long treatment in one of the back rooms? Pandi could've come in for a haircut and left within twenty minutes. This meant I wouldn't have had a chance to see him. Having excluded Phyllis, it also meant either Max or Jock would've styled his hair. It was certain they would've recalled Pandi as a client.

On top of which, his name wasn't an easy one to forget. Max verified that. Repeating Pandi's name a hundred times 'cause he liked the sound of it. *Why me?* But Max hadn't known Adia's last name, and it was obvious today was the first time he'd met Pandi. So he couldn't have been the one to cut his hair.

That left Jock. I scanned the book, confident I'd spot Pandi's name. I guided my finger down the pages. Patty. Penny. Paula. *Drat.* Monikers of all the beautiful women who'd recently stepped foot in the salon with names beginning with *P.* Zilch on the name Pandi. Zero on Gupta.

I slapped the book shut and plunked myself on the stool, wheeling myself back and forth. What had I missed? If Pandi hadn't been a customer, and I couldn't recall seeing him before today, the only way I'd heard of him was remotely through word of mouth. Likely through another customer. But who?

I snatched an emery board from the drawer and filed a nail, thinking of more angles. *Enough of this, Valentine. You have other things on the agenda.* My stomach did a flip in anticipation of the *other things.*

Putting my thoughts on hold regarding Pandi, I replaced the emery board, sprinted to the back door, and felt my bag for my keys. Damn things. Always falling to the bottom. I scoured the inside of my two-ton sack and finally yanked out the sparkly *V* on my keychain, coiled around a headband I'd worn Thursday. I freed my keys, and with a sigh, dropped the headband back in my bag. I really had to clean out this thing. Yeah. Later. When I wasn't playing Lara Croft.

I shut off all the lights, undid the deadbolt, and stepped out into the dark. The instant my heel hit the pavement, I heard a rustling in the bush to the left of the door. At least I thought it was from the bush. What if someone was prowling to my right behind the Dumpster? Or beyond in the parking lot? Call me chicken, but after my assault by Malton and then my recent encounter with the globe,

I wasn't thrilled about playing the hero in hopes of finding a villain.

Gulping down a swallow, I backed into the shop, pulled the door tight toward me, and snapped the lock in place. I peered out the glass, an owl watching for movement—suspicious or otherwise—from the parking lot to the bush.

I fiddled with my keys, berating myself for being edgy. What did I expect to find? A big round globe dancing around Friar Tuck's creaky, spinning-donut pole? Absurd. Even if the mascot had left the park and followed me here, how would it have maneuvered behind a steering wheel? Or get out of a car without plopping to the ground? The visual itself was comical.

As far as Malton was concerned, he was lucky he could walk upright after Romero handled him. Even so, I didn't like the uneasy feeling I had whenever I thought of him.

Several minutes passed. Except for a car pulling out of Friar Tuck's, all seemed calm. Okay, I couldn't stay here all night. Besides, I had a park to return to. I gave myself a short pep talk that all was safe, took a daring breath, and crept back outside.

With my senses on full alert, accounting for each noise and shadow, I twisted around and locked the glass door. I was applauding my powers of observation when a cat leaped from behind the Dumpster with a piece of donut in her mouth.

I jumped back and clapped hand to chest, exhaling loudly at the cat for scaring me. She seemed more frightened than I was, and after a short hiss, she took off at high speed. Good idea. Just what I planned to do.

I pulled the key from the lock, and out of the blue, a chilling presence surrounded me. My initial thought was that the cat had come back. But that didn't explain the change in the air or the anxiety climbing my spine. Staring at the glass door inches from my nose, I saw a slight shadow move behind me. I tried to squeal, but I was paralyzed with dread, my vocal cords seemingly useless.

My pulse pounded in my head, and I squeezed my sparkly *V*, cursing myself for not staying put inside the shop.

In one swift move, my assailant lunged for me. Fight or flight, I thought, not stopping to think of my actions. I lifted my knee and stabbed my spiked heel down on his foot. Simultaneously, I thrust my hand back and jabbed my pointy *V* in his pelvis.

I found my voice and screamed like a madwoman. At the same time, my aggressor shrieked, doubled over, and dropped something to the ground that neither clattered like a gun nor smashed like glass. I was a beat away from running for my life, but I wasn't done with this jackass. Ignoring his cries, I reached for the first thing I could grab in my bag.

Argh. My measly headband. Thinking fast, I whipped it out, tossed my gear aside, and yanked the thug's arms forward. I wrapped the headband around his wrists, looped it over his hung head, twisted it once, and hauled him to the door. I secured his head and hands to the handle, surprised at how light he seemed. I didn't want to choke him to death, but at this point, it was either him or me.

My heart was thumping so fast, my adrenaline in high gear, I didn't stop to check who I'd tied to the door or bother to examine what he'd dropped on the asphalt.

Gasping for air, I stumbled back in the dim light from Friar Tuck's parking lot. Hastily wondering what *had* fallen, I squinted at the ground for his weapon.

Huh. Nothing but a big clear bag of...donuts?

I swallowed in surprise and gaped from the bag to my young assailant wearing tights and a medieval tunic. Judging from the side of his face that wasn't squashed to the door, he resembled the pimply kid who worked at Friar Tuck's. And he was moaning in pain.

"Austin?"

"Yeah?" he croaked out of the side of his mouth.

I let out a huff and quickly unleashed him from the door. "What were you trying to do? Scare the wits out of me?"

"No. *Never.*" He shook his head fiercely, then clamped his neck with an *ouch.*

"Then what were you doing sneaking up on me like that?"

Slowly raising his hands in surrender, he bent with a straight back to pick up the bag. Then he stood there, knees trembling, bag high.

"Austin, put your arms down."

He gawked from my heels back up to my face. "Are you going to step on me again?"

"Only if you keep your arms up."

Like a flash, he threw his arms to his sides.

"What's that you've got there? Looks like a bag of day-old donuts."

"It is." He tossed it at me, clearly still nervous I'd do something crazy like shout *Boo.*

"You'll have to fill in the blanks for me, Austin. Why were you creeping up on me if all you wanted to do was give me a bag of donuts?"

"They're not for you. They're for Phyllis."

"*Phyllis.* Why are you giving her a bag?"

"She called the store today and said something about having terrible indigestion, and it was all our fault. My boss told me next time I see her to give her a free bag of day-olds."

I launched my headband toward my bag in disbelief. Figured Phyllis couldn't wait 24 hours to put in a complaint because of her upset stomach.

He motioned to Daisy Bug. "When I saw you pull up, I wanted to get this off my hands before my shift ended." He rubbed his eyebrows that had finally grown back after Phyllis had bleached them white. "I'd rather not give those to her myself."

I couldn't blame Austin. If I'd been him, I would've moved to another state after Phyllis's experiment, especially after she'd turned him into a mini Colonel Sanders. "Gotcha. I'll deliver them first thing tomorrow."

His head drooped. "Thanks, Valentine."

The day was nowhere from being done, and my anxiety level had barely returned to normal. If this incident was any indication of what my impending mission would hold, then I was doomed.

I told Austin that delivering Phyllis the donuts was the least I could do. After roping him to my door like a helpless calf, I meant it, too.

Chapter 11

By the time I pulled into my driveway, I had a low-grade headache and aching arms. Tackling Austin hadn't been in the plans, but I couldn't blame that for my entire well-being. I slid a look to my hefty passenger, almost forgetting she was there. All right. It wasn't my idea to cart a twenty-pound statue around the park. As for the headache, my mother had a point. I hadn't eaten enough today. That, mixed with my recent upset, likely explained the throbbing temples.

Between Ellie's feet were the donuts I promised to give Phyllis tomorrow. Sure, I could've nabbed one for a quick fix, but that would've been wrong. Plus, I didn't want to deprive Phyllis of her rightful gain.

Deciding to leave the donuts in the car overnight, I put them out of my mind and waved across the street to Mr. Brooks, pruning a shrub into what mirrored a fortune cookie. Mrs. Calvino, next door to me, watched the action from her porch while she puffed on a cigarette with the vigor of a world-class athlete. Rounding off our current ethnic clan was Mrs. Lombardi in her Crocs and housecoat of many colors. She slowed by my house on her nightly stroll with her French poodle, Chester.

I lugged Ellie out of the car, conscious of Mrs. Lombardi's self-righteous glare on my back. I pivoted slightly and offered her a kind smile. "Evening, Mrs. Lombardi."

She halted like a brigadier general, her steel-gray hair uncombed as always, her hold on Chester's leash, tight. "What's that you've got there?"

You'd think having a priest for a son, Mrs. Lombardi would possess a gracious heart. Heck, I'd settle for a beating heart.

Chester wound his fleecy body through her wishbone-shaped legs and gave a fierce bark.

Right. I hefted Ellie over my shoulder, giving up on the niceties. "It's a watchdog."

"A *watchdog*. What kind of crazy—"

In one loud *vrooooom*, Mr. Brooks geared up the chainsaw. Shucks. Just when I was looking forward to Mrs. Lombardi's reproach.

I slammed the car door, hollered *sayonara* to Mrs. Lombardi, and hiked up the front porch, leaving her slack-jawed on the street.

Home sweet home. Once inside, I shed my heels, flicked on my jeweled lamp, and locked the door. Okay. Bohemian drapes, glittery pillows, and overstuffed furniture didn't shout Taj Mahal, but the diverse look suited me fine.

"Well, Ellie?" I gazed into my recent buy's black eyes. "Welcome to your new home."

Talking to a wooden statue was right up there with yakking to flat irons and combs, but no one was around to question my sanity. And if Ellie wasn't complaining, I was in good shape.

I placed my weighty friend on the pine floor in the living room beside the black beanbag chair and hung my bag on her tusks. Immediately, her head did a nosedive to the floor.

"Very funny." I set her straight and lifted the straps off her head. I admitted it. My bag was a tad heavy, thanks to my tools. Probably another reason why my arms were sore. But it never occurred to me to travel without them.

Plus, more important to have everything at my fingertips. My tussle with Austin was proof of that.

I set my bag by the piano and gave the ivory keys a longing look. Nothing would suit me more than to hammer out the stress and frustration from the day. But there wasn't time to brush up on Beethoven. Plus, I wasn't sure I could compete with Mr. Brooks's roaring chainsaw outside.

I called for Yitts, my black cat, and figured fresh food would bring her out of her sleeping spot. I added niblets to her bowl, and she appeared at the bedroom doorway, blinking drowsily up at me.

"Hewwo." I knelt, head low, and she walked over and gave me a head butt.

Then she raised her nose and sniffed toward the entrance. Aha. Something new in the neighborhood. Without giving me or food another thought, she walked gingerly over to Ellie, stopped to assess the situation, then scrutinized me over her shoulder with a *what's this?* look.

Smarty-pants.

I crawled on all fours and sat beside Yitts, petting her head. "This is Ellie. Your new roommate."

Yitts looked from me to this monstrosity three times her size, and I knew what she was thinking. *Who asked for a new roommate, and how's this going to affect me?* She stood on her hind legs, front paws on the statue, and sniffed the wood left and right. Then she jumped onto Ellie's back, circled around, and sniffed some more. Deeming Ellie wasn't a threat, she did a bit of kneading, then settled herself lengthwise, curving her front paws over her new friend's tail end.

Pleased the introductions had gone well, I darted into the bedroom and rummaged through my drawers until I found my black, fitted, 3/4-sleeved boatneck top and 3/4-length black tights. I stripped out of my dress and into the slinky outfit. Then I slipped into my black, ballet-type, foam-soled shoes. Not quite the ballet slippers I'd owned when I attended Miss Lacy's Ballet Studio as a kid, but they were a cute, sparkly replica.

I flung my dress into the clothes hamper, pulled my hair back into a sleek ponytail, and ambled into the kitchen, already knowing what was going to greet me. A big fat nothing. No buffet. No leftovers. No day-old donuts. I would've stocked up on groceries after work, but I had to get to the park, pronto. Yeah. Look how that turned out. I would've been better off spending my day in the produce aisle, feeling up plums and kiwis.

I was deciding on a bowl of cereal or peanut butter and crackers when I heard a knock on the front door. It was a wonder I heard anything with Mr. Brooks's chainsaw whining across the street. Plus, it was going on ten. Who'd be knocking at this hour?

I trekked back into the living room as the chainsaw gasped its final goodnight. Hallelujah. Massaging my temples at the sudden silence, I peeked out the window. A Harley-Davidson sat in the driveway, and Jock stood on my front porch in a T-shirt and jeans, holding a plastic bag.

"Good grief," I said to Yitts who'd leaped for safety and was poking her head out from behind the couch. "What does *he* want?"

She didn't seem to know, so I swung open the door to find out. "If it isn't Thor."

He leaned against the doorframe, setting the plastic bag on my little mosaic table by the entrance. "Thor?"

I swallowed at the image he made and backed off before he saw the appreciation in my eyes, or worse, he picked me up and kissed me. Jock had been in my employment for the better part of a year, and he still had the power to make my nipples harden every time he entered a room. He stared down at my breasts, aware of this, too. Darn Argentinean god.

"Forget it." I let him into the house and raked my gaze from his magnetic eyes down to his clothes, which upon closer inspection were dusty and dirty.

I couldn't remember ever seeing Jock in grubby clothes. Leather, bike clothes, yes. Salon, work clothes, sure.

Swashbuckling clothes, navy clothes, check, check. Pool clothes, *cough*, uh-huh. *No* clothes, *choke*, affirmative!

I slid my gaze from his waist up into his eyes, struggling to appear normal, when in reality my blood was gushing through my veins from the summoned images. "What happened to today's kilt? Plaid not doing it for you anymore?"

He moved in and wrapped his hands around my waist, making me feel smaller than my five-four frame. "You know what would do it for me."

It wasn't a question. And I wasn't sure he was looking for an answer. Yet his exotic leather and citrus aroma, mixed with his natural sweat, spiraled around me. Before I liquefied to a puddle, I blurted the first thing that came to mind. "A Big Mac, small fry, and cherry pie?"

He lowered his head to my neck and planted a small kiss at the base of my jaw. "Not even close. But as you're curious about my kilt, Miss Valentine, I'd say you're wondering if it's true what they say about men who wear them."

I gasped. How dare he try to read my thoughts. The cheeky…know-it-all…

Okay, he was right. That was *exactly* what I was wondering. Suddenly not feeling so plucky, I tried to respond, only my voice box wouldn't oblige. Second time that had happened tonight. Clearing my throat and patting my neck also proved futile.

He grinned, thoroughly enjoying the moment. "Let me help you out. Your first thought is probably whether men in kilts make better lovers." He furrowed his brows in a sincere show of concern, but he didn't fool me one bit. He waited before answering, antagonizing me to no end. "And to that, you'd have to find out for yourself. Now…" he continued, biting back the grin, "if you want to know if men in kilts are handsomely endowed"—he jerked me in at the hips, his gesture primal—"you already know the answer to that."

A high-pitched squeak escaped me.

His tone was low, hypnotic, his eyes soft as they met mine. "But maybe you're just curious whether men in kilts wear boxers underneath. And since you saw me in that kilt today, I'll let you be the judge."

My mouth was hanging open, yet I was incapable of snapping it shut. Visions of Jock in his kilt, a king among men, handling that caber, had me internally sighing with pleasure. And darn him for not giving a straight answer on anything.

"But back to your first question. I had a job to do today, and I had to ditch the kilt."

"Job?" I shook off the daydreaming and backed out of his arms.

"Yeah."

I wanted to ask if this was related to hair, but he swiped the bag off the table, pressed it into my hand, and headed for the bathroom. "Mind if I take a quick shower? I was on my way home, but my shower's on the fritz. Help yourself to the meal."

Shower? Meal? I went to protest, but he shut the bathroom door before I could collect my thoughts.

Of all the nervy…brazen…

Wait a minute. I peered down. What was in the bag? Whatever it was, it smelled delicious. I looked from the bag back up to the bathroom door. A second later, the shower started. Right. I gulped back visions of Jock soaping his magnificent…kilt-less…body in my modest shower and tramped into the kitchen. I wasn't about to let good food go to waste.

I took several warm containers out of the plastic bag. Mmm. Chicken Pad Thai, Chow Mein, and egg rolls. Where had this come from? The fair? Last I'd heard, from Phyllis, Jock had somewhere to go, as in he wouldn't be back. Did this *somewhere* have something to do with the job he referred to?

My mouth watered at the sweet, spicy smells. Food would definitely cure my headache. And he did say to help myself. Anyway, the minute he was out of the shower, it was *hasta la vista, baby*. I had places to go.

I devoured a bit of everything and licked my lips clean when the bathroom door creaked open. I peeked around the corner from the kitchen and almost swallowed my tongue at the sight of Jock sauntering toward me in nothing but my bath towel. It was slung low at the waist, and he was clutching a knot in front with his firmly defined hand.

His shiny hair was slicked back, and his bronze skin glistened while beads of water trickled down his massive chest, disappearing into the towel. "Hope you don't mind me using this." He tossed his grimy clothes from his other hand to the front door. "I didn't want to rummage through your cupboards."

I snapped my jaw shut, realizing too late I'd been gaping. "You're welcome. I mean—" What did I mean? Right now, I couldn't even see straight.

The job, you dope. Ask about the job.

Of course.

I stuck up my chin, a powerhouse of control. "This job. Was it related to work?"

He smiled at that, then wordlessly closed the distance between us, leaving me little option but to either stare at his pronounced nipples or up into his gorgeous face. *Lord, he was infuriating.* Anyone else would've given a short explanation. Not Jock. Peering into my eyes, he laced his fingers through mine and draped my hands around his toned, bare waist. "No."

"No, what?" I couldn't even remember what I asked. And why was the room so hot?

"No, the job wasn't related to work." He took the back of his large hand and brushed it across my cheek. "My turn to ask *you* a question." He tilted his head down at my black shoes and appraised the soft lines of my outfit all the way up to the wide collar on my boatneck top. "What are you up to in this crafty getup? All you need are two pointy ears and whiskers, and you could be Catwoman. In fact"—he pressed his ear next to mine—"I think I hear you purring."

Oh boy. *Was* I. "It's not a cat outfit. It's…it's…"

He backed up a hair and straightened. "It's what?"

I was having a hard time concentrating on anything but his glorious aroma and the hardness pressing between my thighs. *Think, Valentine.* If I told him I was going back to the park, he'd try to talk me out of it, or worse, notify Romero. The two men seldom acknowledged each other at the best of times, the tension between them evident, but when it came to solving crimes, they became superheroes in cahoots. "Ballet! I'm going to ballet class."

The wary eye. "At ten o'clock at night?"

"It's for shift workers." What was I *saying*?

He studied me a moment longer. "I thought you took ballet as a kid."

"I'm taking it again." I did a plié on the spot. "Brushing up. Never know when you may need it."

His mouth twitched into a grin in a way that implied he knew *just when* I may need it. He pulled me in again, a towel the only thing hanging between us.

I wriggled out of his grasp. "You have to stop doing this."

"Doing what?"

I struggled to put conviction in my voice. "*This*." I flapped my hand between us. "Showing up like this. Making the moves."

"Making the moves?" Now he was mocking me.

I planted my fists on my hips, determined to set things straight. "You know Romero and I are dating."

He reached for my hand again. "I don't see a ring on your finger."

I shrugged out of his warm hold, my resolve weakening. "One doesn't need a ring to be committed."

His eyes darkened in a sensual manner, a look that always stirred me. "I see it in your face…in your voice…in your body." His prodding gaze settled on my breasts again, which, damn it, were aching from his hungry stare. "I believe you *are* the type who needs a ring to be committed."

Was I? Had Jock seen through me? Seen something I wanted to keep hidden? Yes, I longed for Romero. But why was I continually pulled in by this Hercules? I'd had my share of Mr. Universe-type men to know this attraction wasn't just physical. Jock possessed something more that drew me in, made me yearn for him, made me forget my vows. I folded my arms across my breasts, gathering a confidence I didn't feel. "You're wrong."

"Am I?" He probed my face with extreme force. "Until I see that ring, I'll be here...waiting."

I felt naked under his touch, sure my legs were going to give out. I couldn't remember when I'd been so turned on.

I wrestled to clear my head. Hadn't I been this aroused a few hours ago when I was in Romero's arms? *Holy mother of God.* Was I willing to sabotage what I had with one spectacularly hot cop for a flash in the pan with Jock? "Why are you here, anyway?"

"I told you. I had a job today."

"What kind of job?"

"Masonry work."

"Now you're a mason?" That explained the dusty heap by the door. "Any other tricks up your sleeves?"

He glanced down at his bare, muscled arms. Uh...yep. I gulped at the suggestive look he gave me.

"When I left Pandi's," he continued, "I stopped at Mr. Wu's Wok for a bite to eat. Thought I'd share with you since it's your favorite Chinese restaurant, plus, it was on my way home. And with my shower not working, figured I'd borrow—"

"Wait a minute. Back up. Pandi?"

"Yeah. Pandi Gupta. Remember, I left work early last Saturday to help him put the finishing touches on the stone entrance of his latest hotel. I should have it wrapped up soon."

"You mean Gupta's Getaways? The one that looks like the Taj Mahal?"

He chuckled low. "That the name of it? Sure."

Of course. That's where I'd heard Pandi's name before.

Jock had said he was doing work for a local businessman. Naturally, Jock being a man of mystery, I didn't stop to ask exactly what kind of work. To be truthful, I wasn't sure I wanted to know. "Your friend may be a suspect in Woody's murder."

"Woody. The guy found at the pond?"

"You don't miss a thing." Sarcasm came out at the worst times.

He raised a sexy eyebrow, and if I knew Jock, I was going to pay for that comment later.

"So they're questioning Pandi because of his partnership with Woody," he concluded.

"You knew about that?"

He nodded. "Their collaboration wasn't a secret. Plus, I saw them in conversation at the hotel a few times."

"Had they been arguing? Was there any discord between the men?"

He grinned and folded his arms in front. "Me thinks Miss Valentine is on a manhunt. The question is, will she find her man?"

With everything that had transpired today, I was in no mood for one of his double entendres. Sneaky. Hunk.

He looked me up and down in my cat—er—ballet suit, and I could've sworn I saw the wheels turning. Well, I wasn't one to kiss and tell. I was on a mission tonight, and the only way I was going to get to it was to throw this man out of my house.

I made another reference to ballet class, pushed him to the door, and stuffed his clothes in his hands.

"Aren't you forgetting something?" He widened his stance, my towel barely clinging to his huge naked form.

Clothes. I came to my senses. "It's certain *I* don't have anything that'll fit you."

He smiled and went for the doorknob. "I've got a fresh change in the saddlebag. Give me a second."

"No!" I lunged for the doorknob. Last thing I needed was for Mrs. Lombardi to spot Jock on my property in a towel and nothing else. She'd probably call the cops.

And if Romero found out, that wouldn't be pretty. Romero showing up at my door, asking what Jock was doing here half naked, would be akin to skydiving without a parachute.

"*I'll* get your clothes." I ducked outside, rushed back in, and threw his duds at him. "Hurry. I can't be late."

He changed in the bathroom, came out a moment later, and accepted the plastic bag I dumped in his hands.

"Thanks for the meal." I shoved him out the door. "It was scrumptious."

"Glad to have obliged." He stopped and turned around. "By the way, I like the elephant. It fits here."

The man didn't miss a thing.

I waited until I heard his bike roar away, then gathered my things, dimmed the lights, and caught the fuchsia gem on Ellie's forehead glow in the shadows. Just like the mood ring. A shiver tore through me, and I spun from escaping Jock's advances back to thinking about the ring and its significance.

Was there any truth to my assumptions on that piece of jewelry? Could Adia have given it to Woody? Did it have a role in his murder? Or was it all in my head?

I went for the door. There was only one way to find out.

Chapter 12

It was after eleven and deadly quiet when I arrived at the park. I didn't see any police vehicles and figured the dive team had wrapped things up hours ago. I'd ask Romero later if they'd dredged up anything. Whether I got a concrete answer was another matter, but I wasn't going to worry about that now. I was here to do my own investigation.

I cruised through the parking lot and passed a few vehicles left from the day. None I recognized, and all were empty except one with steamed up windows, occupied by a couple making out.

I crawled out of the lot and decided to leave my yellow Bug on one of the side streets. No reason to draw attention to myself. In the dark shadows on Cedar, I found a spot along the curb between a pickup and a van.

I took a few moments to gather my wits and monitor the neighborhood for unusual behavior. Other than a Mrs. Lombardi-type in a robe, walking her dog, everything looked peaceful. Telling myself I wasn't crazy for returning to the park, I took a deliberate lungful of air, hitched my bag on my right shoulder, and hurried over one of the footbridges to the fairgrounds.

Since the pond had been the main focal point today, I wasn't going to blow time there looking for clues.

The cops had had enough manpower, and Candace, to boot. My time would be better spent poking elsewhere, like the vendors' booths.

I hiked down a winding path and spotted the softly lit gazebo in the distance. Unexpectedly, a tide of emotions flooded me, leaving me choked up and misty-eyed. This park had helped me when I'd faced my deepest fears, had been there for me when no one else could. It was the one place I trusted through difficult times.

Funny how those thoughts had surfaced now. Memories I hadn't visited in forever. Memories that hadn't been totally erased. Time had lessened the ache but never totally banished it. Yet I'd come through it, whereas a lot of kids hadn't. My love for this park ran deep, and I had to protect it like it had protected me. Max was right. Everyone needed a place to feel safe.

I dabbed my eyes and marched on, more determined than ever to solve this case. Suddenly, a fuzzy image shifted in the dark behind some trees. I stiffened and blinked through the lingering tears, gauging the area closely for more movement. I got diddly-squat. Whoa. I was so edgy I was hallucinating.

I had to get a grip. The park was deserted. Everyone had called it a day. I just had to focus on why I came here. And that was for clues. This brought to mind my assault by Malton MacGregor. He was hiding something. I could feel it. Which was why his booth was the first stop on my list.

I wriggled through the international booths' metal gateway and dashed along in the moonlight, taking note of everything while sniffing the lasting food aromas in the air. I turned a corner and recognized it as the lane where Romero had helped his mother in the Italian booth.

A flicker of warmth spread through me at the memory of him in his apron, but I didn't waste time swooning in the blackness of night. I didn't like dark places at the best of times, and my nerves were ratcheting up with every footstep.

Shaking off the eerie feeling of being alone in the park, I crept along the left side of the row…just in case there were any bogeymen out in the open. If I had it right, another fifty feet, and the Scottish booth would be on my left.

I kept my head up, making out the tops of canopies in the moonlight. Aha! The crown of a blue-and-white tent told me I'd reached my destination. I tiptoed in my ballet shoes to the edge of the stall and froze, listening for sounds, peeking over my shoulder for good measure. Nothing stirred. Not even a mouse.

Scolding myself for trying to be witty, I squeezed my bag to my side and slinked through two counters squashed together as an overnight closure. Didn't seem like much of a deterrent for intruders, but I guess they weren't worried about someone stealing a pound of haggis in the wee hours of the night.

Okay, Valentine. You're here. What are you looking for? That was a tough question. One I didn't have an answer for. But if my feelings about Malton were correct, I needed to see if there were any clues in his booth, something that would pin him as Woody's murderer.

I patted my way along the counter, bumped into a hat stand, and tripped on a fat cloth bag with knobby arms. The bag gave a shrill hum, then a puckered wheeze. I yelped and fell back in alarm, hands to the ground. *Sheesh.* I blinked at the lumpy thing in the darkness. Just a bagpipe, giving me a heart attack. Probably one played earlier today by one of the men.

I silently cursed my stupidity, then had a brainwave. I had a flashlight on my phone, didn't I? Last time I needed it for a case, I'd been knee-deep in dirt outside Rueland Retirement, shoveling my way out of another mystery.

I pulled my phone from my bag, clicked on the light, and aimed it at eye level at the shelves in front of me. Paper bags. Empty cash box. Tape. Wax paper. Crumpled pack of cigarettes. Empty beer steins. Ha. Likely from this afternoon, when Candace went to cheer up the Scots.

Judging by the number of steins, looked like she'd made several trips.

I flashed the light around the booth. Hmm. Nothing else of interest. Only fair-type goods and souvenirs. I leaned over and surveyed the glass fridge, not ruling it out as home to a clue.

No luck. Zero signs in the fridge.

I slumped back on my butt and plopped the phone on my lap. *Shoot.* Wasn't there anything here other than what you'd expect at a multicultural fair? The answer to that was obvious. The more I thought about it, why would Malton hide something in the booth? If he'd killed Woody, nothing like waving a red flag.

I got to my feet and toed something under the counter. I didn't squeal in pain, but the sturdy tap told me the item wasn't a particularly light object either. I pointed my phone down and shone the light by my foot.

The edge of a wooden paddle poked out from under the counter. And I couldn't be sure, but was that *blood* on the blade?

I stifled a scream, shoving my fist in my mouth. My heart thrashed around in my chest, and I was momentarily woozy. This had to be it. The murder weapon, a.k.a. the canoe paddle we'd been searching for.

Deep breath, Valentine. In and out.

I gave myself a second to come to terms with what I'd discovered. Not letting fear get in the way of snooping, I calmed my beating heart, crouched down, and examined the tip of the blade. I reached to slide it out from under the counter but instantly threw back my hand, hearing Romero's warning about touching a piece of evidence with my bare fingers. Okay. Becoming a skilled sleuth took time, especially when impulsiveness made me jump in with both feet. I was learning, wasn't I?

I plucked a sheet of wax paper off the shelf and used it to nudge the paddle out.

Wait. What *was* this? It wasn't a canoe paddle after all. It was much shorter…and the paddle was more rectangular.

My eyes widened. This was a *cricket* paddle. And cricket paddles were used for playing cricket. Furthermore, it was India's most popular sport. Just so happened India was represented at the fair this weekend. It would also seem I'd met a possible cricket player who went by the name of Pandi, who also happened to be a business partner to Woody—the victim.

Yikes. Didn't Kashi say he and Pandi played in the same sports club? Granted, he didn't specify it was cricket they played. But judging from the green-and-orange jersey Pandi had worn earlier today, I was willing to bet he was indeed a player.

My mouth filled with a bitter taste while ugly notions flooded my brain. Was it Pandi who'd been arguing with Woody at the porta potty? Suppose they'd been disputing about work, their partnership, or something more. Then what if Pandi shrank back from sight when Tantig hobbled up?

Details weren't my great-aunt's strong suit. She hadn't been sure if it'd been a man or woman quarreling with Woody, and she couldn't decipher an accent. Tantig probably couldn't tell what day of the week it was. But she did observe Woody's ring glowing red. A sure sign of anger, if one believed that stuff.

At the time, I suspected it had been Malton arguing with Woody, but what if it had been Pandi? Did Pandi kill Woody with a cricket paddle, then plant it at the Scottish booth to implicate one of Woody's clan members?

A cricket game had been in full swing when I first arrived at the park today, though I couldn't be sure if Pandi had been playing. In fact, I hadn't even met him until several hours later. But if he *had* played, and his paddle—the apparent murder weapon—had been safely concealed, who was to say he hadn't employed another paddle? Who was to say a player even brought his own paddle to a game? I wasn't familiar with the sport, but if it was anything like baseball, there were always spare bats for players to use.

All this speculating on Pandi seemed airtight, but a nagging feeling sent my thinking back to this booth and Malton MacGregor, the number one suspect on my list.

Let's say Malton knew through conversation with Woody that Pandi was a cricket player. Did he steal Pandi's paddle, kill Woody, and leave it here for safekeeping? Or plan to plant it in another spot later, to point suspicion elsewhere? That part I couldn't be sure of.

A sudden memory of Malton skulking behind Pandi's tent today sprang to mind. Was he slinking about just to scare me? Or was he staking out the area in hopes of slipping the paddle into Pandi's tent when no one was looking? With the cops questioning everyone, he would've had to get rid of the evidence.

Yowza! Officer Martoli had even questioned the Scots at this very booth, unknowingly standing a mere four feet away from the paddle, if it was even under the counter at the time. Maybe that was why Malton had acted aloof when Martoli was here. Didn't want to appear like he knew anything. Which brought up motive. He was already notorious with the police. Why risk injuring his reputation further by killing Woody? For financial gain? Because of jealousy? Hatred?

My head was spinning from all the theories. In addition, what about Hoagy MacEwen? He was another enigma, one I wasn't going to eliminate. I glanced down again at the paddle. Main thing tonight was that I had proof to give to Romero. And I'd do that on my way home.

I switched off my light, stuffed my phone back in my bag, and peered over the counter. With no bogeymen in sight, I swung my bag over my shoulder, gripped the paddle with the wax paper, and tiptoed out of the booth. The next site on my list was the porta potties.

The unappealing commodes had been set up all over the park. Just because I wouldn't use them didn't mean I'd overlooked their locations. However, the one Tantig visited, according to my mother, was stationed behind their stall. I wasn't sure what I'd find there, but I wanted to check out the area for myself. Maybe there'd be a clue in disguise.

Letting the moonlight be my guide, I veered past the row of stands that included the Armenian booth and plodded across the dewy grass until I was face to face with the teal outhouse. Two outhouses to be exact. Side by side. Plus, there were several tall shrubs, an evergreen, and a birch tree, all in reaching distance.

I stood there, tapping my right index finger on the wax-papered paddle, assessing the area. Where would I hide if someone came along and I didn't want to be seen bickering with Woody? I did a lap around the porta potties, marking my steps cautiously around the trees and shrubs.

Interesting. No less than three hiding spots for anyone wishing to disappear swiftly. That didn't include inside the other porta potty. But considering the freedom of movement the culprit seemed to have, and Tantig not mentioning any noise coming from the other porta potty, I ruled it out, going on the premise that it had been empty. To my estimation, whoever had quarreled with Woody either hid behind one of the bushes or trees, or at the rear of the units.

I trekked back to the front of the structures. With my left hand, I wiggled the handle on the first outhouse. The door opened smoothly and was empty. I gagged back the smell wafting out at me and hastily shut the door. No need to search further.

I sidestepped to the second outhouse and jiggled the handle. Stuck. I tugged on it some more, but it wouldn't give. Yep. This had to be the one that wouldn't open for Tantig. That is, until Woody had come to her rescue.

Since I wasn't getting anywhere with my left hand, I switched the paddle into my left and jerked the handle good and hard with my right. Come *on*. How hard could this be? I was putting more weight into my wrenching when something grabbed my attention.

I froze, coming back to my surroundings, my fingers gripped in place. Was it my imagination, or was it just a distant cry from a bird? A car cruising a side street? The rustle of the wind?

Pinpricks traveled down my arms, and I slowed my breathing. The question I feared most bubbled to the surface. Was someone else here in the park? I forced myself to think rationally, choosing not to get worked up for nothing. And the rational answer was that there could be a night worker at the fair. A custodian sweeping garbage or cleaning stalls.

I gulped back that thought with doubt. Wouldn't I have run into someone by now? Heard the swishing of a broom or the scraping of garbage cans? Wouldn't I have noticed lights?

I squinted over my shoulder and steadied my nerves. I had to calm down. There was no one in sight. I was alone. I found the porta potty Tantig had used, and I had the paddle. The day's events were simply getting to me. There were no other noises, and I wouldn't be satisfied until I looked inside the outhouse. I took a deep breath, and with a surge of determination, I rattled the door again. After a good yank, it finally released.

Before I could congratulate myself on my strength, I was shoved into the porta potty from behind, the paddle was ripped from my hand, and the door was slammed shut behind me.

"*Aaaaah!*" I stumbled over the toilet and clasped the germy walls, righting myself before falling headfirst into the hole—or worse—the urinal. I shot my hands back and spun around. "*Hey!*" I banged on the door. "Let me out!" I pounded some more and kicked the door with my soft ballet shoes. Lot of good that did. Something must've been wedged through the handle on the other side.

My stomach lurched from the rank smell floating beneath me, and panic rose in my throat. I booted the toilet lid down, overcoming the stench, but the dread from being stuck in this standup coffin was building. Me and tiny spaces weren't a good combination. Added that it was night and I was on my own only escalated things.

"*Help!*" I pounded the door again, giving into the panic. "Anyone there?" Sure, someone was there. A killer. What did I want? A signed note? "*Hellllp!*"

I was hyperventilating and losing control. *Breathe*, I ordered myself. Slow and easy. Getting hysterical wouldn't do any good. *Think*. Who locked me in here?

I didn't have to think. I knew. Malton! *Ooh*. I was rammed in here so abruptly, I couldn't recall if there'd been a hint of cigarette smoke. I bit back my screaming, put my nose to the door, and sniffed along the frame. If Malton were my attacker, I'd catch the odor. Drat. Nothing.

Sensational. I'd had a bona fide clue to give to Romero, too.

I leaned my ear to the door and listened for any commotion outside. No movement. No sounds except for a dog barking in the distance. And the damp grass would've been a silent cushion under my assailant's feet. I chewed on my lip, thinking things through.

One thing was certain. I wasn't staying in here for long. I almost plonked my bag in the urinal, then swiftly swung it into the tiny sink and rummaged for my phone. Romero would come to my rescue. I stopped short and reconsidered my actions. Was I in the mood for a lecture? For I-told-you-so? Uh-huh. Nix that idea. My parents were out, too. I'd never hear the end of it if my mother thought I was in danger. Twix and my sister both had kids. I couldn't drag them out of bed at midnight. That was if Holly was even *in* bed. As a vice cop, she worked absurd hours like Romero. Which made calling her a worse idea. I didn't need her contacting him, thinking she was being helpful.

I could call Max, my faithful servant. But who knew where he was at the moment? And if I took him away from Princess Jasmine, I'd regret asking for his help.

Crap. Who did that leave?

A bead of sweat trickled between my breasts, and my heart leaped around inside. I had no choice but to call Jock…if he was even home by now. He lived in Cambridge, which wasn't exactly a hop, skip, and a jump away, but he'd do anything for me—or he would've until tonight's earlier conversation.

Phooey. How did I get myself into these situations?

I switched on my phone and waited for it to come to life. I waited…and waited. What the heck? I clicked the side button again. Nothing. What was suddenly wrong with this thing? I clicked it one last time when it struck me. Max had reminded me earlier that I had 18 percent left on my battery. I insisted I was going to charge it when I got home. *Grrr.* I could be a real doofus sometimes.

I drew a hefty sigh, swiped a stubborn tear that had popped out, and came to terms with my predicament. I had no option but to save myself. I ditched my phone back in my bag and pressed my hands on the door. If only I had a can opener. I was being ridiculous, but I wasn't built like Hercules, like *some* people, and I didn't have the know-how to bust through doors like *other* people. All the same, the structure resembled lightweight plastic, nothing that a few good bangs with a sturdy object wouldn't break.

I dug out my blow dryer, the heaviest item in my bag, and whacked the butt at the door handle. The door didn't budge. Okay, in theory this should've been easy. I kept hacking away and moved onto the hinges, putting some muscle behind it. Then I gave the door a few good blows with my shoulder, rocking the entire unit a smidgen. It felt like I was pushing a boulder uphill with a teaspoon, but I wasn't giving up.

By now, sweat was pouring down my temples, and adrenaline was coursing through my veins. I wiped my forehead, heaved a deep breath, and gave the door one last shove. The hinge broke off the top, and I stumbled out into the fresh air and into a huge wall. A huge *leather* wall. For a second, I was stunned with fresh panic. "*Jock!*" I didn't know whether to laugh or cry.

"You rang?"

I exhaled with a shiver, accepting the warmth and security from his leather-clad embrace.

He smoothed my head to his chest. "I thought my Spidey senses were telling me something."

I pushed back. "What's that supposed to mean?"

He stiffened into a no-holds-barred pose. "It means, you think I bought that ballet-class story?"

I was glad for the darkness because I was sure I was turning beet red. "Yes?"

He dragged me a foot away from the porta potties. "Lucky for you, I wasn't born yesterday. And before I ratted you out, I figured I'd check out the park to see what you were up to. Only *you* would snoop at all hours the night of a homicide."

"Bully for you. You found me out. Now where's the paddle?" I whirled around and combed through the shrubs, hoping whoever had nabbed it had accidentally left it behind.

"What paddle are you talking about?"

I heard his words, but something caught my eye near the porta potty door. I rushed over, crouched to the ground, and swept the thick branch aside that had obviously been stuck through the handle to keep me locked in. Then I uncrumpled the item. Grand. Nothing but the wax paper.

I got up and shoved my hands on my hips. "The murder weapon! I found it at the Scottish booth. There was even blood on it. But whoever locked me in the porta potty took off with it."

He nodded. "We talking a canoe paddle?"

"No. A cricket paddle."

"You mean a bat."

"*Yes.* A bat."

While he thought about this, I darted inside the outhouse.

"Funny time to take a leak."

I scowled back at him. "I'm not taking a *leak*." I dumped my blow dryer inside my bag and hooked the whole damn thing over my shoulder, pointing to it for good measure. "I forgot *this*, if you didn't know."

Having enough of my sauciness, he wrapped his arm under my butt, hoisted me over his shoulder, and carried me toward the exit. "You should be thoroughly spanked for disobeying orders and coming back here tonight." He set me down with a thud.

I gave an indignant tug on my top, staring up at him with steely-eyed conviction. "Who have you been talking to? Romero? You two working the same side of the street these days?"

His voice was stern. "Let's just say we both want to keep you safe."

We finally reached Cedar Street where I'd left Daisy Bug, and where Jock's Harley was parked two vehicles behind. On the outside, I was acting bold, when in truth I was more scared than I'd ever been. One too many frights. One too many failures. "None of it matters now since I no longer have any evidence to give him."

A wave of exhaustion washed over me, making me weak and trembly. "Plus, I…I can keep myself safe."

A tear rolled down my cheek, and I defiantly swiped it away. How was I going to prove I could be tough and solve this murder when I couldn't control my emotions? Worse, I couldn't even hang onto a piece of evidence.

He pulled me in and rocked me in his comforting arms. "Shh. I know. You're a pint-sized Wonder Woman."

I sniffed back the tears. "And don't you forget it."

Chapter 13

I woke early the next morning with so many things going through my mind, I had no clue where to start. I'd called Romero last night when I'd gotten home and left a message about finding the bloody cricket paddle. What he did with that information was his business. I just thanked the stars above he wasn't available to take my call. And doubly grateful I'd dodged the inevitable shouting match at an ungodly hour of the night.

As it was, I'd tossed in bed, unsure whether to blame my restlessness on the case, Max's rekindled friendship, my feelings for Romero, or Jock's…Jock's what? I didn't even know how to label what this was between us.

I'd wasted enough time brooding. If I wanted to see this case through, I needed to get back to the park and continue my hunt for a killer. First thing today, though, was a visit to Gupta's Getaways.

I wasn't about to eliminate Pandi as a suspect even though Malton was at the top of my hit list. I'd been certain Malton was the one who'd pushed me into the outhouse last night, but what about the absence of cigarette smoke? This was reason enough to question Pandi today. And he *had* told me to come by, hadn't he? If this was the last hotel where Woody and Pandi had been working, I wanted to see what I could unearth.

I searched my bag and dug out the card Pandi had given me. Hmm. Harbor Street. Definitely the touristy part of town, also one block away from several other hotels. I tucked the card back in my bag with a plan of sorts forming in my head.

I brushed and fed Yitts, then showered, combed my hair, and examined my eyes. After ripping off my idiotic false lashes yesterday, it didn't hurt to double-check that my own lashes were still intact. Being weary last night, I'd hardly looked at myself after scrubbing my face clean. I leaned into the mirror and blinked left and right. Glory be. No signs of lash loss. My mother would be pleased I wasn't joining Sheila Kunkel's daughter in the missing-lash club.

I ate a bowl of Raisin Bran, chugged a glass of pineapple juice, then brushed my teeth and spread on some makeup, going easy on the mascara. No need to give my lashes another tough workout.

Since I'd already let my mother down yesterday by not helping in the booth, today I'd be somewhat available. At a minimum, I'd be in costume. This would make her happy.

I groped through my closet until I found my traditional Armenian gear. *Ahh. Yes.* Creatively tailored by my own hands. I smiled inside. Perhaps I'd look like I just got off the boat next to my mother and great-aunt, but I'd be the one with extra sparkle lining my bodice and wearing one layer of lace fabric instead of three.

I zipped into the long, flowing red skirt that hugged my hips and pulled the glittery scarlet top over my shoulders. I twisted my hair high on my head and placed the matching cylindrical headpiece snugly on top, letting dozens of small coins frame my face.

I slipped on my finger bracelet and cuffed a silver wristband on each arm. Feeling thoroughly made up, I gave myself a squirt of Musk, inhaled the flowery aroma with pleasure, then did a final tally in the mirror. Perhaps I didn't look as striking as Adia in her delicate Indian sari, but this was a close second.

My coins jingled when I bent to give Yitts a kiss goodbye, but she didn't mind the intrusion or the mist of perfume that showered her. I yanked on my trekhs, the Armenian version of loafers, which were the only part of the outfit I loathed, then grabbed my bag and checked my fully charged phone for messages. One, and it was from Romero. Too bad I didn't have time to listen to it now. I'd call him back later, like next year, when I was certain he'd had time to cool after digesting my news.

Telling myself I hadn't done anything wrong by snooping around the park last night or finding the paddle, I plunked the phone in my bag, locked the house, and carried myself in my ugly loafers down the porch to my car.

I cut across town, hopped onto Montgomery, and sailed by Rueland's candy factory, the Peanut Gallery. I lowered my window a crack, enjoying the aroma of fresh peanut brittle instead of the scent filling the car from Phyllis's sticky donuts. Driving on, I passed Dino Hosta's, Rueland's haven for the rich and famous, and turned onto Harbor Street.

Nearly blinding me in the morning sunlight was a beautiful white hotel, outdoing all the others, with round domes and a lavish entranceway. If Dino Hosta's was the most luxurious hotel in Rueland, Gupta's Getaways had to be the most exotic.

I slid on my shades to block the sun, then stopped the car at the hotel entrance. Oh boy. Jock. What was he doing here? I didn't think he'd be working on a Sunday. He was in jeans and a black Harley-Davidson T-shirt, and he was crouched on the stone walkway, scraping something off the ground.

I zipped into a parking spot, threw Phyllis's donuts in the backseat out of the sun, and gathered my skirt, exiting the car. I approached Jock from behind, taken in, as usual, by his focus on the job. Probably why hundreds of women loved being in his salon chair. That, and the fact he made them look and feel like consummate beauty queens.

He scrubbed the porous granite with a rag, his wide shoulders tensing as he worked his muscles back and forth. Keeping my thoughts on the task at hand, I stopped three feet from him and fought the tickle in my nose from the pungent solvent he was using.

I squeezed my nostrils to stifle the itch, but it was no good. "A-*choo*!"

Jock swiveled around, a look of surprise on his face. "Bless you." He dropped his rag by the yellowy stain he'd been scrubbing, then got to his feet and stretched his arms over his head. "You're up early," he said, taking in my outfit.

"Didn't sleep well last night," I confessed, sliding off my sunglasses.

He gave me his sexy hiked-up eyebrow. "Any reason in particular?"

"Don't flatter yourself." I avoided his hot stare, which at the moment was working through my thin layer of clothes. "The case is simply playing on my mind."

He nodded in understanding. "So you thought you'd dress up like a tantalizing mistress and check in at the hotel for a good sleep."

I tapped my shades on my palm. "Not exactly. Since the multicultural fair isn't open for a few hours, thought I'd motor over here and check out the place. Pandi told me to visit." I produced the card he'd given me as proof.

Jock's slow nod told me he knew I was full of it. "So now you've visited, off you go. The festivalgoers will want to get a look at you in that outfit." He reached over and fingered one of the medallions on my forehead, his voice taking on a sexy tone. "If you stay here, I may not be responsible for what happens next."

Not going down *that* road again—or giving up on my search—I brushed away his hand with the card and took a casual look around. "Is he here?"

"Who? Pandi?"

"Yes."

"Nope. And I don't expect him to be."

I sliced him a suspicious look. "What do you mean by that?"

"Nothing." He crouched again and continued scrubbing the smudged walkway.

I scrutinized the yellow stain bleeding into white. "What happened here?"

He grimaced. "One of Pandi's hired hands spilled his paint can this morning on the way to his van. I was here doing my job and told the guy to leave it. He was all thumbs. Figured rather than have another accident, I'd clean it myself."

I grinned, recalling someone else I'd met who was reportedly all thumbs. "He sounds like the Cutlers' friend I met yesterday at the fair."

He chuckled. "Short? Chubby? Mid-thirties? Has a face like Elmer Fudd?"

"I was thinking Porky Pig. His name is Emery."

"Yeah. Emery. Said he had to scoot to the park, so I offered to clean up the mess."

As always, the knight in shining armor.

Slipping the card back in my bag, I glanced at the huge archway leading into the hotel, my thoughts way ahead of me. "If Emery had been painting here, do you think he might've noted strange behavior between Woody and Pandi?"

Jock shrugged. "Couldn't say. But if I know you, you're going to find out."

I huffed out a sigh. Nothing wrong with having an active mind. And no better time to put it to good use. I slid on my shades. "Correct you are."

Jock could tease me all he wanted. Today was the last day of the fair, and if the murderer wasn't caught before the end of the day, it'd be next to impossible tracing clues and witnesses once everyone had dispersed from the park.

Not bothering to point out the clock was ticking, I gave a small curtsy, twirled around in my long skirt, and sprinted to the car. I'd show *him*. Mr. Masonry.

I arrived at the park at nine, an hour before opening. With so much on my mind, I'd forgotten about Phyllis's donuts in the backseat. Oops. I'd get them to her sooner or later. Frankly, she wouldn't bat an eye at the day-olds that were getting older by the minute.

I passed vendors opening their booths and setting out products for the day. I nodded and said a few hellos while I searched for Emery. Might as well ask the Cutlers if they'd seen him since he'd helped them yesterday.

I'd left my sunglasses in the car and squinted in the morning sunlight as I hustled to Betty and Birdie's canopy. They were easy to track. Stationed behind their counter, their cheery voices chirped over the quiet rumble of nearby vendors setting up.

"Blimey!" Betty ceased from laying out shortbreads iced like British flags and double-decker buses. "Look who's here!"

Birdie looked up from setting out napkins. "Valentine! Don't you look *ravishing!*"

I gaped down at myself, forgetting I was in costume. A preoccupied mind did that to you.

Giddy with delight, Betty remarked on my finger bracelet, and Birdie swooned over my lace outfit. Before I knew it, they'd left their stall and were springing to my side, their awe spreading to the intricate design on my skirt and coins on my hat.

Not wishing to extend the greeting any further, I thanked the sisters for their kind words and steered them back to the reason for my visit. "Is Emery here today?"

Birdie pointed toward the Ferris wheel. "I believe I saw him chatting with that big cuddly globe. But Emery'll be back soon. He's helping us start today."

"That's okay. I'll find him." I backed up a foot. "I hate to run, but I've got things to do before opening."

"Cheerio!" they sang in unison.

I jogged toward the midway and spotted Emery and

the globe standing together, facing my direction. Not wanting to appear anxious, I slowed my pace and bid a friendly air as I approached them.

"Hi, Emery. It's me, Valentine." I thumbed my chest in case he didn't recognize me with the cultural garb covering nine-tenths of my body.

He hiccupped a chuckle. "Hey, Valentine. I'd recognize you anywhere. You're so pretty, you're hard to miss."

"That's very sweet. Thank you."

"And hey"—he pulled at the hem of yesterday's red T-shirt that was now splotched with yellow paint—"we could be twins."

I gazed from his stained T-shirt to my red outfit. "Yes, I imagine we could be twins."

He really was a sweet guy even though I questioned his affinity for yesterday's clothes. But I wasn't here to judge his fashion sense. Furthermore, the paint stains were confirmation that Jock and I had been talking about the same guy.

The globe, that had been standing still, raised its puffy white-gloved hand, tapped Emery's shoulder, and waved goodbye. After nodding at me, it skipped away.

Curious about the mascot's identity, I turned to Emery. "Friend of yours?"

He tugged his shirt down over his belly. "Not really. She's just another fair worker."

"She?"

"Yeah. They need people small enough to fit in those silly getups. And she felt she couldn't be bullied in a costume, so this was right up her alley."

"I'm sorry." I clicked my tongue in sympathy. "Bullying's a tough thing to endure." Childhood memories of being harassed haunted me, but I'd never escaped those nightmares through veneers. Of course, that hadn't stopped my tormentors from imitating *my* appearance, painting their skin olive, donning long, dark wigs.

Emery nodded. "Yeah. She's not really a kid, but I suppose people get bullied at all ages."

I narrowed my eyes on the globe, now a speck in the crowd, my mind stuck in the past. I'd matured, left school, and gotten a life. I wasn't sure I could say the same for those female bullies.

Emery lifted one shoulder in a shrug. "I'm sorry, Valentine, but the Cutlers need me to help open today. Was there something you wanted?"

Darn. I didn't want Emery to get away without asking about Woody and Pandi. "Yes. Sometimes I do a little sleuthing for the police. This weekend especially, since the homicide." That was two lies in one breath, but it was all for a good cause. "I just came from Gupta's Getaways and wondered if you'd mind answering a few questions."

He blushed. "Shucks. Am I in trouble over the spilled paint?"

I gave him a charitable smile. "No. But I did run into Jock cleaning the stonework on the walkway."

"Jock?"

I spread my arms high and wide. "Superman without the tights."

He giggled. "Ohh. Jock. Yep. Great guy."

"Yes. He mentioned you'd been painting the hotel for Pandi."

"Among other things." He dipped his head humbly. "I installed their computer program. Call me a geek. But they were also having trouble with their paint contractor, and since I'm a bit of a jack of all trades, I offered to help."

"I'm sure they appreciated that." I dropped my bag by my feet, rolling my shoulder in relief. "When you were there working, did you ever hear or see Woody and Pandi arguing?"

He crossed his arms over his tubby belly and looked up at the sky in thought. "Nope. Can't say I ever did. But I once saw Pandi's daughter fighting with Woody."

"Adia?"

"Yes. She poked him in the chest like she was taking a stand about something. Didn't look too happy to me."

"How long ago was that?"

He scratched his chin, calculating. "Few weeks ago?"

"Could you tell what the fight was over?"

He shrugged again. "Might've been related to the business, but I'm not sure." He scanned the time on his phone, then did a hop on the spot. "Sorry, Valentine, but I have to go."

"Sure." I smiled through a frown. "Thanks for your help."

He went to slide his phone in his pocket and dropped it to the ground. He bent over to pick it up, then rushed off. I stood there for another moment, attempting to isolate what he'd said that was bothering me. I squeezed the bridge of my nose, forcing myself to think, but I was getting nowhere. Maybe my snug headpiece was cutting off the circulation to my brain cells.

I adjusted my headgear, then gave my shoulder another roll, wincing from the ache. Next time I wouldn't use it to bash a dumb outhouse door. Nothing more I could do about that, I picked up my bag, turned my back on the midway, and hurried toward the international booths.

Time was marching on. The park would open shortly, and I wouldn't be much help at the Armenian stall if I wasn't there. At best, I could get a start preparing individual cartons of tabbouleh and hummus for those wishing to take samples home.

I waited on a forklift ahead of me, delivering more kegs of beer to Candace's tent, and sensed a presence behind me. Bracing myself for the worst, I clutched the straps of my bag and twisted around cautiously.

"Whew." Just Max, my sidekick. I closed my eyes briefly and relaxed my shoulders. "I can't tell you what was going through my mind."

Max stood with his arms crossed, a stony look covering his adorable face.

"What's wrong?" I joshed. "You not get enough sleep last night? And why didn't you respond to my text? You're always nagging me for not using my phone. Then when I use it to contact you…I get crickets."

He cut me a disgruntled look, which left me feeling strange. Here I was, standing in my ethnic dress from head to toe, and Max had nothing to say. At a minimum, he could've commented on my coined headpiece. A remark. A joke. A Max wisecrack. Nothing.

"Maybe you should learn to type," he said, not what I'd expected.

Before I had a chance to clarify, he whipped out his phone. "And I quote, 'Leach in psych. And goon hoop.' What the heck is a leach in psych? And who's the goon?"

"I know how to type. And that's not what I said." I sighed in aggravation. "What I *said* was, 'Leaving the park and going home.'" I looked him squarely in the eye. "And if you hadn't been busy stargazing with you-know-who, you would've figured that out."

He sighed back at me. "If you must know, I wasn't stargazing with Adia."

I winked, trying to lighten the mood that was turning more somber by the minute. "What happened? She stand you up?"

"Not exactly." The way he avoided my stare said he wasn't thrilled talking about it. "When I got to the Ferris wheel, she wasn't there. I waited awhile, and she finally texted saying she forgot she had something to do, and she'd meet up with me at closing."

I mulled this over. "Okay. So you still had your date."

"It wasn't a date, and anyway, it got cut short." The strain around his eyes suggested he'd either had a tiff with Adia, or he was put out with me. And the way my gut was roiling in pain from his indifference, I was leaning toward door number two. "Max, are you mad about my text?"

He gave me a cold glare. "Let's just say I had a rude awakening."

"Can you be more specific?"

He tightened his lips and shoved his phone back in his pants pocket. Then, as if overcome by emotion, he threw his hands in the air. "How *could* you!"

I lurched back in surprise at his tone. "How could I *what?*"

I prided myself on being astute, but I didn't have a clue what he was angry about.

The hurt in his eyes stung me to the bone, making things worse since I couldn't come up with a reason why he'd be this irate. I rewound things to what transpired between last night and today, and…

Uh-oh. Lightning bolt to the brain. The message I hadn't listened to from Romero. What if it was in response to my message *to* Romero? The one about me finding the bloody cricket paddle, the cricket paddle I assumed belonged to Pandi. Somewhere along the line, trouble must've struck the businessman, which in turn concerned Adia…which obviously affected Max.

I swallowed a coarse lump in my throat, my knees weak. I was the cause of the hurt and disappointment in his eyes. "Max, what happened? Tell me."

He sniffed, his nose out of joint. "The police took Pandi in for questioning. Said they had grounds to believe he killed Woody. *Somehow* it came out that Pandi's cricket paddle had been found, and now they're doing DNA tests and Lord knows what else in hopes of proving Pandi's a murderer." He paused. "Why do I have the feeling it was *you* who found the cricket paddle?"

Found it…and then lost it. Were the police performing tests based on hearsay? Or had the paddle actually been discovered again?

I squeezed my lips together, afraid if I opened my mouth, I'd say the wrong thing—even if it was the truth.

Max looked so broken, his sorrow speared me to the heart. By all accounts, it seemed he was becoming more fond of Adia. If he continued to rekindle this friendship, and Adia's father was convicted of murder, that wouldn't bode well. I tried to imagine how I'd feel if I'd been in his position, but I had no idea where to begin.

He took a difficult breath. "I can't believe you took Romero's side over our friendship."

I could barely look Max in the eye. It was evident he felt betrayed, but I had to set him straight. He'd want that if he were thinking clearly. "I'm not taking sides, but it's possible Pandi could be a killer. Have you thought of that?"

He put his chin up, and though there was a glimmer of uncertainty in his eyes, there was no mistaking the clarity in his words. "I've thought about a lot of things in the last few hours. Most of all, work. You'll have my resignation in the morning."

Chapter 14

"**M**ax." The notion of him quitting over my part in this was so absurd, I wanted to scream. "You can't be serious."

"I've never been more serious." He stiffened, then stalked away without looking back.

The park gates had opened, and people were pouring in. The last day of the multicultural fair was officially underway. But it was all a blur. Flashing lights. Blaring music. Baking smells. Everything muddled together, and I couldn't enjoy any of it due to my heart being trampled on.

A single tear ran down my cheek. This was uncharacteristic of Max. I could understand his compassion for Pandi and Adia. But could he have been that far gone to ignore the truth? To take a stance against me? Against the bond we'd had all these years?

I couldn't allow him to leave without…without what? I stopped in my tracks and straightened. What had I done wrong? Led the police to a killer? Had Max forgotten I'd caught his friend Freddie's killer, a.k.a. Ziggy Stoaks? Twice? Murder was murder. Plain and simple. Max was acting like a hypocrite. Still, I felt awful.

Let's say Pandi was found innocent, and the real killer was arrested. This whole thing would blow over, and Max would forgive me. But in order for that to happen,

I had to keep searching for clues. The cricket paddle had pointed to Pandi, but maybe there was something I'd missed.

I called Max again. Rushing past people, I caught up to him in the grassy field where Phyllis's yard-sale table had been. Skimming the area, I briefly wondered what had happened to it. And where was Phyllis? I looked up in silent plea, trying not to agonize over her affairs. Forgetting about Phyllis for the time being, I lunged for Max's arm.

He whirled around and tapped his toe, giving me the courtesy of hearing me out.

"I promise," I said, my chest tight with grief, "I'll dig for more clues. If they're only questioning Pandi, there's a good chance they'll let him go. Especially if he has a solid alibi."

The steely edge in his voice softened, and his shoulders slackened. "We'll see."

It was the best response I could hope for, considering the situation.

A strained truce ensued, neither one of us broaching the subject of work. Thank God for small mercies. I'd almost lost Max once before. I didn't want to picture life in the salon without him again. I couldn't get rid of Phyllis if I tried…and I had, yet here my amigo, my sounding board, my Steady Eddie was slipping through my fingers.

In a small part of my soul, I wondered if I was worried that Adia was replacing me. No. That was ludicrous. My insecurities or feelings for Adia were immaterial.

We offered each other a feeble smile, wading through tense waters, when Phyllis plodded up to us in a long, golden orange-tiered skirt and a red cropped blouse with tassels dangling at the midriff. Her hair was wrapped high, mirroring the poop emoji, and she was adorned in gigantic hoop earrings, garish rings, and gold bangles. Long scarves draped from her waist, and in her raised hand was a large, half-eaten salted pretzel. I was so shocked at her appearance, I completely forgot to mention her donut inheritance.

"If it isn't Gypsy Rose Lee." Max had withheld from noting my outfit. *Now* he chose to let loose. "What, no more Fat Bastard?"

In outrage, Phyllis dropped her arm, gasping from Max to me, her bangles clanking at her side. "Did you hear what he called me?"

I spied Max out of the corner of my eye, his expression on Phyllis, blasé. As much as I hated him wrangling with her, I would've overlooked it this once to see the familiar mischief in his eyes, to see his mood lifted. I got neither. "I don't think he meant it meanly, Phyllis. He was referring to a Scottish character in an Austin Powers movie."

"A character who is a fat bastard," she corrected.

"Forget it," Max said. "This swirly getup suits you. In fact, I want to take that point on the top of your bun and spin you around 'cause you look like a giant spinning top."

"Good!" she barked. "That's what I was striving for. A giant spinning top."

I sighed at Max, then gave Phyllis my attention. "Can we focus on more important things? Like how are you feeling today?" I scanned the area again. "Plus, where's your table?"

"And tambourine?" Max piped.

Phyllis hiked up her skirt to her navel. "I don't *have* a tambourine."

"Harmonica?"

Oh brother.

Phyllis gave Max a sharp glare, then dismissed him like roadkill. "If you want to know"—she wagged her pretzel at me, bits of salt sprinkling to the ground—"it may have been more than an upset stomach yesterday. I may have had a heart attack after all. And it *could* happen again."

Instantly, the donuts I needed to give Phyllis came to mind. I opened my mouth to tell her about them, but it was futile.

"You're not going to have a heart attack, Phyllis," Max said. "Stroke, maybe." As always, empathetic to the core.

"What are you getting at?" she asked.

Max gestured to her half-eaten pretzel. "Only that you're doing a bang-up job rethinking your eating habits."

Phyllis swung her gaze from Max to her pretzel and back to Max. "I had to have *something* for my ten-o'clock snack."

"What are you having at eleven? A side of beef?"

She scooped the scarves in her hand and squeezed the life out of them, likely dreaming of strangling Max. A shimmer from one of her scarves caught my eye, and upon closer inspection, I noticed gemmed barrettes and suspiciously familiar hair extensions tacked to them.

Not sure what Phyllis was up to with all the decorations, I abandoned my fixation on the scarves and intervened before things got worse. "Who said it may have been a heart attack, Phyllis?" As of yesterday, it was deemed indigestion. When did it go from stomach cramps to cardiac issues?

"Nobody." She gawked at me as if I didn't have a brain in my head. "I figured it out for myself."

Max touched his chin in thought. "Why don't you figure out how to spin yourself away like your nonexistent yard-sale table."

Didn't surprise me that Max had also noted Phyllis's missing stall. The most unobservant human would've spotted the gouges in the ground where her station had been.

"I ditched the yard-sale idea," Phyllis grumbled. "People are so cheap. They want everything for nothing."

Not sure how I could argue that with Her Royal Highness of the Bargain, I waited for her to expound.

"So today I'm selling these silk scarves." She flailed the jeweled scarves back and forth like a matador baiting a bull. They kept snagging on her tassels, and she repeatedly flicked them away.

"Uh, Phyllis…" I motioned to her scarves. "Where exactly did you get all these hair extensions?"

She puffed out air, then coughed, like she was stalling. "Where do you think I got them?"

"We know you didn't buy them," Max stated. "You're too cheap for that."

"As a matter of fact, I *didn't* buy them." She turned to me. "They were sitting in an old box at the shop. I figured they were only going to go to waste, so I took them off your hands."

Too stunned to speak, Max dropped his jaw and wheeled his head from Phyllis to me.

"*Phyllis...*" I tried to remain calm, which was becoming increasingly hard since I didn't know if my frustration was really directed at her or from my row with Max. "That *old box* was designed to look that way, and you could've asked first."

She shot her hand down in one firm stroke. "Yeah, yeah. And you would've come back with some sob story how you were saving them for the hospital kids."

At least she acknowledged my Monday visits with the sick kids where we played my beauty game, Mon Sac Est Ton Sac. "That's not what they were for. I have a client coming in next week who I specifically ordered those hair extensions for."

Her eyes bulged out. "So order more."

I stuck my nose in her face. "Those were from *Italy*. I special-ordered them."

"Pff. I saw the same ones at Walmart. You can get them on your way home. She'll never know the difference."

Before I could reprimand her, she signaled across from where she had been stationed yesterday to a table heaped with colorful scarves. "These ones are perfect for my creations. Even did a demonstration already on how to wear them. I'm all set up over there. And look! There goes my model."

We swiveled our gazes to a guy bumping into tables, a beige scarf wrapped around his head like a mummy, arched hair extensions bouncing from his scalp.

"Oh, look. King Tut meets Captain Jack Sparrow." Max shook his head at Phyllis. "Another happy customer.

I'd like to stay and feel sorry for your next client, but you'll have to excuse me. I need to fill in for Adia."

"Who's Adia?" Phyllis wanted to know.

Max gave an exaggerated sigh. "An old friend."

"That Indian girl running the jewelry tent? So *that's* who I've seen you cavorting around the grounds with."

"First of all, Phyll, I don't cavort. Secondly, they sell more than jewelry in her tent. And thirdly, not that I need to share anything with you, but yes, I've been spending time with Adia."

Getting things back on track, I turned to Max. "Why are you filling in for her? Where is she?"

"I don't know. She called me this morning and asked if I'd open the tent for her. Sounded like she had another job to do."

What other job? I didn't want to push Max, but I had a lot of unanswered questions. First, from my chat with Emery. More since I'd met up with Max. I cut my focus from Phyllis's latest catastrophe and traced back to something Emery had said earlier—or not said—that kept niggling me.

"*What?*" Max waved a hand in my face, interrupting my thoughts. "You look bothered. It can't be because of Phyllis stealing the hair extensions. You'd have already gotten over that shock."

"Hardy-har-har." Phyllis swatted Max with her scarves.

He stood rooted, waiting on an answer from me. What could I say? I couldn't fit the pieces together to explain what was going through my mind. But something didn't feel right; the thrashing in my stomach confirmed it.

"It's nothing." I pushed Max away. "Go. It's after ten. You don't want to let Adia down."

He squinted at me, knowing me too well to leave this for long. "Talk to you later then."

He spun around, and my heart gave a heavy thud. "Yeah."

"*Much* later." Phyllis raised a stiff middle finger at Max's retreating back, her bangles jangling, her rings glinting in the sun.

"Uh, Phyllis?" I reached for her hand, momentarily distracted. "Where'd you get this ring?"

She flapped her hand this way and that. "Which ring?" Good question, since there was one on each finger.

I motioned to the mood ring on her middle finger, glowing red. No surprise, after the last few minutes of feuding.

"I bought it at what's-her-name's tent." She poked her head in Max's direction.

"You mean Adia's?" I'd neglected thinking any more on the mood ring Woody had worn and the display case full of them in the Indian tent.

"Yeah."

"When did you do that?"

"I don't know. Late yesterday when my yard sale flopped."

Interesting. There'd been an hour or so around suppertime when Max and I had looked for clues before he trailed off to meet Adia at the Ferris wheel. We'd even witnessed Candace slogging out of the pond when she'd been looking for *her* clues. Probably when Phyllis had wandered into Adia's tent.

"I don't know what he sees in her." Phyllis cranked her neck toward Max again, then took a hunk out of her pretzel.

Seemed I wasn't the only one with doubts about Adia. But on first appearances, there was no question what Max saw. I blinked wide-eyed at Phyllis. "Have you *seen* Adia?"

"*Yes*," she hissed, spitting a chunk of pretzel to the ground.

"Then you'd agree she's the most beautiful specimen God ever created."

Phyllis bent over, swiped the morsel off the ground, and blew it clean. "So she has a red dot on her forehead. Big deal."

Why did it come as no surprise that Phyllis wouldn't appreciate a thing of beauty? She struggled to make a basic haircut look good. How did I expect her to recognize anything beyond that?

"Phyllis, the dot is called a *bindi*, and Adia wasn't wearing one."

"What was she wearing then?"

I envisioned Adia yesterday in her gorgeous sari. "When I saw her, she had a pear-shaped medallion resting on her forehead. That's it. No dot...I mean, *bindi.*"

Phyllis popped the crumb in her mouth and shrugged like she couldn't have cared less. "Well, she didn't impress me one bit, and I especially didn't like the way she was talking to that Scottish guy."

I pushed my headpiece away from my ear, not sure I'd heard right. "What are you talking about? What Scottish guy?"

"The guy who was there when I bought the mood ring. Keep up!"

Keeping up to Phyllis was like keeping up to a drunk driver. "If you only knew how hard I'm trying. Who was he?"

She groaned. "You think I went up and introduced myself?"

I swallowed to give myself a second before I throttled her. "Okay, Phyllis. Let's start from the beginning. You went to Adia's tent, and you bought the mood ring."

"Yes." She snorted. "Boy, you catch on fast."

I ignored the slight and moved on. "What happened after you purchased the ring?"

"I moseyed into Kashi's tent." Like it was self-explanatory. "He said he saw you yesterday."

"Yes. We had a grand reunion. And you moseyed into his tent *because*?"

"Because I wanted advice. I've seen enough people walking around the park with his 'Get Out of Town' brooches, and I figured it couldn't hurt to get tips on how to make my scarves more appealing."

Of course.

"I'm calling them 'Get the Hell Out of Here' scarves."

What else would she call them? My gaze slid down to her decorative scarves made, in part, with my material.

Reluctantly, I had to give her credit. She was trying to make a go of the scarf thing, and if asking Kashi for guidance helped, then more power to her. "What happened next?"

"While I waited for Kashi to finish up with a customer, I heard angry voices in the other tent."

"In Adia's tent."

"Yes." Anticipating I was coming at her with another question, she hurried on. "So I edged back to the opening of her tent and saw the Scottish guy and Adia going at it. I had no choice but to duck behind a clothes rack and listen to what they were saying."

"Phyllis! You didn't!" Actually, I was impressed with her chutzpah. "What did they say?"

She frowned and puckered her lips. Phyllis's way of thinking. "I didn't hear the whole conversation, but clear as a bell, I heard her say, 'I'm glad he's dead.'"

My eyes felt like they'd popped out of my head. "Are you sure? I mean, is it possible she said she was *sad* he was dead?"

"No, it's *not* possible. I have 20/20 hearing," she professed, mixing her phrases. "And after a coughing fit, the Scottish guy grunted, 'Wishes sometimes come true.'"

The feeling in the air shifted. "Coughing fit? Did the guy have a cold?"

"No. It was a smoker's cough. Regardless of that, he was a gorgeous specimen himself."

Malton MacGregor. I was certain of it. He must've had his chat with Adia, then lurked around the Indian tent, attacking me after my spider calamity with Pandi.

"Did it evolve into a fight? You said they were going at it."

She scrunched up her nose, ruminating on this. "I didn't know what to make of it. At first, it sounded like they were in collusion over something. Then they were blaming each other."

"For what?"

"I. Don't. Know." She gave a pouty look down at her

rings. "They were arguing about why she gave some guy a mood ring."

"What guy?"

She shook her head, frustrated. "Do I look like a psychic? Kashi called my name, so I whipped around and slid back into his tent. That's all I heard from the other two."

I took a heavy breath, processing all this. Not only did an aura of suspicion surround Adia, but now the stakes had been raised. Now it appeared she wasn't in this alone.

What's more, the origins of the mood ring had finally surfaced. There was no doubt Adia had given it to Woody. If I assumed correctly, Malton must've caught wind of the mood ring flying off Woody's finger, since anyone could've seen it. Another reason why he possibly threatened me. He was afraid I'd draw a connection from Woody's ring to the rings in Adia's tent, then to Adia. Was this why they'd been arguing?

This led to more questions. Did the two plan Woody's death? Could Adia have lured Woody to the pond where Malton had been waiting with the cricket paddle?

Phyllis had given me a lot to think about, triggering one thing in particular, something Romero had said about Woody's murder. Maybe he was right. Maybe it wasn't a woman who'd clobbered Woody on the head. Maybe a woman was simply the last thing he saw.

Chapter 15

I finally had a chance to tell Phyllis about Friar Tuck's donation and promised to get the donuts from my car later. She grunted in satisfaction, then stamped off to her new table, her "Get the Hell Out of Here" scarves trailing in the grass behind her.

With that looked after, I wanted to scour the park for Adia, if she was even here. I looked down at my clothes. Shoot. It'd have to wait. I had to make good on my vow to help at my parents' booth. I wasn't nuts about doling out tabbouleh when things were compounding in the case, but maybe time working the stall would help me plot my next move. After all, even if I did find Adia, I couldn't march up to her and throw accusations of murder.

Moreover, there was Malton to consider. Whatever I did later, I knew from experience I needed to be careful around him.

I turned toward the food area, mulling over my theory on Adia and Woody once again. If they'd been dating—and by now I was fairly certain they had been—and she'd given him ultimatums regarding his philandering, then it was possible his womanizing led to his murder.

I wasn't acquainted with Adia personally, and I'd only seen her acting sweetly in Max's presence, but I'd worked enough years in the salon to form fair opinions on one's character.

And what I sensed in our Princess Jasmine was an air of privilege. Adia was not someone to put up with anything less than excellence. In essence, she was a woman who got her way.

Despite Romero's dismissal on the jealousy theory, I dug deeper with the information I had. Let's say Adia herself had caught Woody with another woman. Maybe she'd tried to reason with him, first with words, then notes. Concluding he wouldn't change and green with envy, she might've schemed with one of his fellow Scotsmen to take him out. Enter Malton MacGregor.

I couldn't see Adia physically beating Woody to a pulp, but if she'd asked Malton to do the job, why him? It didn't look like they were romantically involved, so what was his vested interest in all this? It was evident there'd been some type of animosity between him and Woody. His attitude yesterday regarding Woody's demise was a dead giveaway. But what would lead him to kill?

I was making a plan to speak to Barn again in hopes I'd get more out of him on Malton when I noticed a mob surrounding a policewoman. Hmm. Was there news on the case? Had Romero sent another uniform to do more investigating? I put my prior plans on hold and inched over to see what I could find out.

I pushed past the throng and halted ten feet from Candace *impersonating* a cop, scantily dressed in a blue uniform like she was this month's *Playboy* centerfold. She had her hair secured back in a tight bun, a toy sheriff's badge on her chest, and handcuffs dangling from her waist. With a pad and pen in hand, she shouted orders to the next guy in line.

"Name. Height. Occupation."

It wasn't clear if she was interviewing witnesses for the case or lining up her next date. The guy in front of her probably wasn't sure either. He couldn't seem to raise his gaze beyond Candace's almost-covered chest. This didn't stop her from firing the next question.

My pulse hammered the way it always did when within

twelve feet of the human devil, but I left Candace to it. I had better things to do. I turned my back to the mob and continued on, breathing a sigh of relief that Candace hadn't detected me. Suddenly, I felt a clawlike grip on my shoulder.

"Where do you think *you're* going?" a voice demanded.

Crap. I twirled around and slung Candace's hand off me. "Isn't it obvious? Away from you, masquerading as a police officer."

"Jealous you didn't think of it first, Valentine?"

I looked her up and down. "Yes. I'm so jealous I didn't think to rent a costume and pretend I'm a cop, I'm going to keep on walking and let you continue your charade."

She shoved closer and poked her pen at my chest. "At least I look better than *you* in *your* costume. Who are you supposed to be anyway? Scarlett O'Hara?"

I glanced down at my slim-fitting Mediterranean attire, confused by the comparison. "Forgive me, Candace, if I don't welcome your sarcasm, but I fail to see a connection to the Southern belle from *Gone With the Wind.*"

She sneered, lips rolled back like a German Shepherd. "You're wearing *scarlet*, aren't you?"

God save me. "Yesss," I said with hesitation. It was beyond me why I ever thought Candace would solve a murder case. She couldn't even deliver a proper insult.

"Boy, are you dense." She took her pen to flick one of the coins on my forehead.

I jerked back, turning the other cheek before she touched me. "I'd love to stand around and take insults, Candace, but your next witness is drooling over there. Plus, I'm needed somewhere else."

"You're not going anywhere until you've answered my questions."

Being in loafers, and Candace inches taller in high patrol boots, I was at a disadvantage from meeting her tough gaze eye to eye. Nevertheless, I squared my shoulders and bit back from laughing in her face. "*You're* going to ask *me* questions?"

"You heard me. Everyone's a suspect." She flung open her pad. "Name?"

I raised my eyebrows, thinking I'd fallen into a black hole. "You already know my name."

"*Name.*"

"Scarlett O'Hara." I slid up my chin and smiled sweetly.

She snapped shut her notepad and stuffed it in her cleavage. "Always the wiseass, aren't you."

"You asking or stating? 'Cause I have more important things on my itinerary than guessing at your questions."

Someone from the crowd tossed a few kernels of caramel popcorn at Candace. "Hey, Officer Hottie, you coming back to grill us, or what?"

"Yeah!" another one shouted. "I'm waiting to be handcuffed."

Candace ignored the bunch and tightened her focus on me. "More important things on your itinerary, like spying, I take it. Like you were doing on me last night."

"Excuse me?"

She folded her arms across her pushed-up boobs and tapped her long red fingernails on her arms. "You heard me. You drove right by Hoagy and me in the parking lot last night."

Last night. Parking lot. I blinked in confusion, then blinked in realization. "That was *you* steaming up the windows in that car?" Who else would it have been? Candace had enough hot air to melt a Russian fortress.

She nodded proudly. "We needed to relax after the day."

"If you had relaxed any more, that car would've blown all four tires."

"Ha. Ha. And here I thought Malton was the only one skulking around the park after closing."

"What?"

"Hoagy and I had…uh…relaxed enough and were leaving the parking lot when we ran into him. Seemed he forgot something at the booth, and he needed to fetch it."

Fetch it, huh? I narrowed my gaze, recalling my ordeal at the outhouse. It *was* Malton who'd locked me in there. *Creep.* Probably came back looking for the evidence he'd stashed.

A bunch of youths swaggered by and asked Candace where the beer tent was. She pointed without thinking to the location that had a fresh delivery minutes ago.

The teens giggled, then took off, and I gawked at Candace in disbelief. "Uh, Officer Needlemeyer, you just indicated the way to a group of underage kids."

She flapped her hand at me, the dense one. "They're asking for their parents. Anyway, about Malton."

Right.

I opened my mouth to pose a question when Hoagy marched up to us and dragged Candace three feet away. He motioned to her getup, rambled on about something, then did a bunch of *achs* and *ayes*. Candace whispered something back, pointed to *my* outfit, and Hoagy muttered some more, aiming his unfriendly glare at me. I didn't have a clue what he said, and I waited, hoping Candace would translate. Go figure. Me, depending on Candace for something.

There was a moment's silence, and finally Candace widened her eyes at me. "Well? You going to answer him?"

I leaned in. "Sorry? Was I asked a question?"

She looked from me back to Hoagy and made an exaggerated sigh as if to say *I told you she was impossible.* Without waiting for a response from him, she turned back to me. "Hoagy's wondering why you're parading around in costume when there's a killer right under your nose."

Me parading around in costume? That was rich. "What are you talking about, Candace?"

"Hoagy thinks Malton killed Woody. What you don't know, Valentine, is that while Woody slept with that little Indian in the sari, he was also sleeping with Malton's girlfriend. Did so for months before Malton discovered their secret."

I was momentarily speechless. "How long have *you* known this?"

She wrapped her arm around Hoagy's shoulder. "Since last night. Hoagy told me after we saw Malton strutting into the park."

"Then why are you interviewing all these people?"

She rolled her eyes at me. "A good detective doesn't take just *anyone's* word."

Couldn't argue that.

Having just insulted *Anyone*, she kissed his cheek and gave him a wink.

I gaped at Hoagy, hoping he'd clarify his theory. He spewed more hard-to-decipher phrases, threw in a boatload of hand gestures, and waited for me to respond.

My eyes widened, and I smiled sheepishly. "Okay?" Perhaps if *I* expanded. "If Woody slept with Malton's girlfriend, you think Malton would've been upset enough to kill Woody." It now made sense why Hoagy had given Malton that scowl yesterday and uttered "Mishap, my arse" when I mentioned Woody's drowning. He didn't think Woody had drowned at all. He'd suspected Malton of his murder.

"Ach. You bet that's what I think," he declared.

Worked up by all this talk, the speed of Hoagy's words flew faster than I could grasp. Candace did some nodding and *uh-huhs* and pursed her lips in contemplation.

Getting impatient, I did a come-on, tell-me motion with my hand.

Patting Hoagy's shoulder in a calming manner, Candace faced me. "Hoagy saw Malton talking to the Indian princess on Friday when everyone was setting up for the festival. Kind of suspicious, don't you think?" She swayed on the spot thoughtfully.

I looked from Candace to Hoagy. "Very suspicious." Were Adia and Malton cementing their plan hours before Woody's murder because they'd both been cheated on?

I shivered from the direction this was taking, and as much as I wanted to move on, I had one last question for

Hoagy. "When was the last time you saw Woody on Friday?"

He scratched his scruffy jaw and frowned. "Ah dinnae ken. Before we went for a bevvy."

I slid my gaze back to my interpreter. "Who went for a bevvy?"

"Hoagy and I," Candace said. "We were together Friday night. Went for drinks after setting up."

I fiddled with my finger bracelet, recalling Candace taking the tray of beer over to the Scottish booth yesterday afternoon. And yesterday was Saturday. "But you only met Hoagy yesterday."

She smiled coyly. "Wrong again, Miss Stupid Sleuth. We met at one of the multicultural fair meetings last month...one you weren't present at."

"I wasn't present at *any* of them." *So there*, I felt like adding. I had no need to be at the fair meetings. My mother had signed up for the Armenian booth. She was the one who enjoyed business gatherings and engagements. I was happy to receive an assigned position. Which I was sorely failing on.

"And *you*..." Hoagy sputtered at Candace, plucking her toy sheriff's badge from her chest and crumpling it in his hand. He broke out in another long speech, and Candace stood there taking it. Seemed Hoagy was none too happy with his girlfriend flouncing around in a dominatrix outfit, mimicking a police officer.

I think I liked him after all.

I left them to their dueling and jogged to my parents' canopy. By now, my mother and great-aunt were there, dishing out kebab and hummus like it was going out of style.

I darted behind the stall and picked up the slack on the tabbouleh, making sure there was lots of pita bread to go around.

"Where's Dad?" I asked, slipping Tantig a kiss on the cheek.

My great-aunt rolled her eyes. "He's home, read-ink the newspap-air."

My mother deposited money from a customer in the cash box, not voicing her opinion on my father's absence.

"He couldn't do that here?" I asked my mother, mildly irritated he wasn't around to help.

"Your father's had his fill of people for the weekend." She lowered her voice and jerked her head to the next booth. "Insulted our Korean neighbors yesterday by asking if their food was any good." She flattened her lips in disgust. "He never learns."

This sounded about right. I was lucky I took off when I did last night. "Don't worry. I'm here."

"You don't have to hang around. Once the rush is over, Tantig and I can manage." She looked from the line of customers back to me. "Any word on the homicide?"

I gave the easy answer. "No."

She eyed me warily, moving on to my outfit and more important things. "Do you have to make everything you wear look provocative?" She zeroed in on my cleavage. "I can't decide if you look like you're going to a cultural gathering or a singles bar."

I looked down at myself. My cleavage was far from showing, but the fact that I was in glitter mode and didn't resemble an actual immigrant from the 1900's may have had something to do with her remark.

"If Romero's too busy to commit, there are lots of men here looking for a beautiful young woman like you."

Oy. Here we go. Why did I tell my mother Romero had been gone so long? A smarter woman would've kept up the charade, pretending to see him occasionally. That was what I got for being honest.

"Lots of *ethnic* men," she continued. "I even saw Kashi Farooq. Remember him? From the Love Boat? That man has a great personality and an enterprising future."

"Yes, I saw Kashi." Not that I didn't want to picture myself as Mrs. "Get Out of Town" Brooches, but now that the line had dwindled, this was my opportunity to escape my mother's matchmaking and get back to the case.

I turned from the fading crowd and gathered more

containers for the next batch of customers when an unexplained force entered my sphere, making me acutely aware I was being watched.

I whipped around and spotted Romero standing a safe distance from our stall, wearing jeans and a plaid flannel shirt unbuttoned over a black Rolling Stones T-shirt. His legs were wide, arms crossed, sleeves rolled to his elbows. He didn't look happy, yet he didn't look mad. I recalled his message that I hadn't listened to, not trusting an outburst wouldn't occur.

I swiveled back around, pretending I hadn't noticed him, doubly hoping he hadn't seen the flush creeping up my cheeks. Why I thought I'd get off lucky, I didn't know. I knew by his intensifying rugged scent that he'd strolled to the edge of the canopy. Waiting.

"Valentine," my mother said in a strained voice. "You've got company."

"No, I don't." I busied myself, heaping containers on top of containers. "It's probably some down-on-his-luck vagrant wanting a handout. Give him some kebab, and he'll be on his way."

Romero cleared his throat, which was never a good sign. "Down-on-his-luck vagrant?"

I whirled around from the sound of his deep voice, a rehearsed shocked look on my face. "Oh, it's *you*. If you want tabbouleh, you'll have to get in line."

"I'm not here for tabbouleh."

"Hummus?"

He extended his arm toward me, palm up in a gentlemanly fashion. "Mind if I have a word with you?"

"Maybe later," I said lightly. "I'm needed here right now."

"She can go," my mother chimed cordially up at Romero.

I slapped the containers on the counter with clenched teeth and glared at Benedict Arnold. "Thanks."

Romero took me by the arm and led me to the back of the stands, fifty feet from the porta potties. One commode in particular was in the process of being replaced by the sanitation company. Romero looked from the busted door on the outhouse to the huge sanitation truck loading the entire thing onto its flatbed, then back to me. "Know anything about that?"

I lifted my eyebrows innocently at the truck. "Looks like a defective outhouse."

"Does, doesn't it? Not sure how an outhouse becomes defective. Maybe you have some theories."

Sensing his eyes on my face, I stuck out my chin, faking concentration. "Nope. Can't think of any."

Since Candace's broadcast that Malton had been in the park after closing, I should've volunteered my suspicions about him to Romero. But I wasn't feeling brave. Might've been Romero's warning clanging in my ears to stay away from him, or the fact that I *wasn't* sure it was him who'd pushed me in the outhouse. Even with mounting evidence, I kept coming back to the cigarette smoke. Wouldn't I have smelled it if Malton had been my aggressor?

I shifted my gaze from the truck to Romero's plaid shirt and put on a bright face, hoping I was making the right decision by steering him in another direction. "You're getting into the spirit of things."

Not amused by the cheery change in topic, he took his hand and scraped it across his unshaved jaw.

I pressed on, ignoring his dominant presence and grim face. "You're wearing plaid, aren't you? Scottish? Tartan? Multicultural fair?"

He glanced down at his clothes. "I'm also wearing a Stones T-shirt, but you don't see me carrying a guitar."

All righty then.

He forged on. "You want to tell me why you returned to the park last night?"

He wanted answers? I'd give him answers. "I told you on the message. I wanted to see what I could find."

"And that, you did. The cricket bat that was smeared with blood—which the lab will confirm was MacDunnell's."

"You're welcome."

His chest heaved, his darkening expression not lost on me. "You know you could've been killed?" His tone was dead serious. "Especially since you had something the killer wanted."

"Well," I argued, "he found it."

"And planted it by the back entrance of the Indian tent."

"Is that where you located the paddle?"

"Bat. Yes. Slightly less bloody than what you'd described."

I tapped my loafer on the ground. "If Pandi were the killer, why would he bring the paddle or bat or whatever you want to call it back to his own tent?"

Romero leaned heavily on one leg and shook his head, undoubtedly wondering how I knew about Pandi. Then he blew out a sigh that said he didn't want to know. "Sweetheart, you've got a lot to learn about the criminal mind. Gupta might've figured he'd clean off the blood and replace the bat in hopes no one would suspect it had been used."

Okay. But what if Adia had been involved? Why would she—or Malton, if they'd been in this together—bring the cricket paddle anywhere near the tent? For the same reason? To clean and replace it before it was detected missing? Or was there a deeper motive here I wasn't understanding? A motive that had to do with shielding a loved one as in, was Adia shielding her father? Or the bigger question. Was Pandi protecting his daughter?

"Is Pandi still in custody?" The question brought to mind my early-morning visit to Gupta's Getaways when I'd seen and asked Jock if Pandi was there. His blunt *no* and remark that he didn't expect Pandi to show up told me he knew more. Clearly, he'd been aware that Pandi had been taken into custody.

Chances were, Jock had turned around last night after depositing me by my car and searched the grounds.

Finding the paddle at the Indian tent, he'd then delivered it to the cops. But I didn't care to get into it with Romero. The two could keep their cloak-and-dagger, espionage secrets between themselves for all I cared.

"Yes. We're not through with Gupta yet. And if his alibis for last night and the night of the murder don't corroborate, we're looking at murder one."

I wanted to explore my theories with him on Adia, but I flashed back to the promise I'd made Max about searching for more clues. Though things were looking bad for Pandi…and Adia, I needed to keep digging. The cricket paddle was obviously the biggest piece of evidence, but maybe I'd skipped something else. "What about the pond? Did your team find anything?"

"Nothing but a few glass bottles and lone shoes nobody's missing."

"And the mood ring?"

He nodded. "I'll give you that. It did belong to Woody."

Phyllis's spying had already confirmed that.

Which had me thinking again…if the ring had been glowing green when Romero's mother had run into Woody, was it possible he'd just stolen kisses from Adia? That would've explained the color that signified romance, according to Twix. Of course, in view of Woody and Adia's crumbling relationship, maybe he hadn't been kissing her. What if he'd been making out with another woman? If he'd been the playboy everyone described him to be, he could've been with anyone.

"What about Malton?" He wasn't totally out of the equation.

"What about him?"

"Woody slept with his girlfriend. I'd say that's a pretty strong motive for murder."

Romero pondered this. "Where'd you hear that?"

"Hoagy MacEwen."

He watched the sanitation truck drive away, then swung his cop glare back to me. "Did you also know that *Malton* slept with *Hoagy's* girlfriend?"

I did an open-mouthed gasp. This evidently accounted for Hoagy's true contempt for Malton. "Doesn't anyone sleep with their own girlfriends?"

Romero lost the hard edge and traced the back of his hand along my cheek, gently fingering the coins by my temple. "I'm trying."

Yow. Stepped right into that one.

His breathing slowed, and he did one of his sexy appraisals that went from my head to my toes. "Do you know what that outfit is doing to me?"

I quivered from the depth of his voice and the indication of his touch, my heartbeat galloping in my chest. "I have an idea."

On the outside, Romero possessed a tough, controlled demeanor. When he was in lockdown-mode mentality, God save anyone who defied him. Yet when the lines softened around his eyes, and his lips swelled ever so slightly, there was no mistaking: this man had a sensual side with emotions that ran deep. Not something many saw.

He took his finger and trailed it down my neck, between my breasts, and rested it at my navel. "I want to see this on you next time we're alone."

I was on fire and wasn't sure I could wait until next time we were alone.

His cell phone rang, and he yanked it out of his pocket, his prolonged stare on me, hot.

"Yeah?" He listened, head down, then did some nodding. "Be right there." He hung up and centered on me again. "Gotta run. There's been a break in the case."

"Wait!" I stammered. "Where are you going?"

"Gupta's Getaways."

"Why? What happened?"

In response, he cupped my face, reached down, and placed his full lips on mine. I should've been ticked he evaded my questions, but his kiss turned ravenous, and his raw desire aroused me in all the right spots. A beat later, he broke off and searched my eyes. "When this is over, I want you."

Gulp. That was a direct order if I ever heard one.

He flicked my chin and backed up. "Stay out of trouble. Hear?"

I gave him a shaky thumbs up. I would've verbalized an *okay*, but at the moment I couldn't find words.

Chapter 16

I stumbled back to the Armenian booth, wondering what Romero's break in the case was about. I could nag him for details till I was blue in the face. It'd get me nowhere. Well, I had my own break...of sorts. While Romero dashed off to follow up on his lead, I'd move forward on mine.

My mother turned from the counter and watched me grab a bottled water from the cooler and down half the contents. "Guess we don't need to find you an ethnic man after all. By the look of you, I'd say Romero's making up for lost time."

She had no idea.

I kept my expression neutral, not wanting to add to her commentary. "Think you're okay handling things from here on in? I have something to do."

She gave me a knowing smile and told me to go. I narrowed my eyes on her, then took one last chug of water. I pitched the empty bottle in the recycling bin, still feeling her stare on me.

"*What!*"

She grinned. "Just glad to know someone is making you happy."

I was sweating from the inside out, my heart was pounding a mile a minute, and I was pretty sure my legs were going to give out from the sexual rush I'd just had. I didn't know what the definition of *happy* was, but by all accounts my physical state was implying *heart attack*. On the chance I survived, I didn't want to suggest my mother hire a wedding planner just yet.

Avoiding more talk on the matter, I looped my bag over my shoulder, told her I'd see them later, and took off for the Scottish booth.

Barn was alone, sorting keychains on the counter when I ambled up. Hallelujah. I had no desire to see Malton. And as for Hoagy, he was another mystery. I could understand his anger toward Malton for wrecking his relationship with his girlfriend, but to accuse him of someone else's murder because of it? That was plain, downright...well, human. Then again, was it possible Malton had killed Woody for the same reason? Cripes. Whoever said understanding the male psyche was easy?

Barn opened his large bear paws in welcome. "There she is. How's our wee Agatha doing? Or should I say Sherlock?"

Most people wouldn't get away with that kind of teasing, but coming from this big man in his kilt and jovial face, I knew there was no mocking intended.

"I've been better." I plunked my bag on the counter and slapped my arms beside it with a mix of exhaustion and frustration.

He leaned in. "Just so ye know, ye dinnae look anything like Agatha—or Sherlock—in that lovely red dress." He winked, his cheeks rosy and plump.

I sighed at that, and his eyebrows shot up in doubt. "Aye, what's on your mind, lass?"

Did I tell him about the break in the case? Was I wasting my time continuing my own investigation? I moaned inwardly. If Romero was onto something, then terrific! On the other hand, what if it was only a false lead?

No sense stopping my search. In fact, what if I untangled the case before the cops? True, I wasn't Agatha or Sherlock, but I had my own ways, and I'd solved cases before. Plus, I'd learned a thing or two since then.

I smiled at Barn and glanced all around, my voice low. "Where are the others?"

He leaned closer and glanced around, too, like he wanted in on the secret. "What others?"

"MacEwen and MacGregor."

He straightened and waved his huge hand down. "Ach, those lads are probably on the chase."

"The chase. You mean, chasing women?" Based on what I'd just learned from Romero, this was becoming a major theme.

"Aye."

"Is that a Scottish thing?" As soon as the words were out, I knew it was a stupid thing to say. I mean, look at Romero with his swarthy looks and persuasive charm. He'd probably win the gold medal of all time for chasing women. Oh, wait. Romero was also half Scottish. *Groan.*

"Ah dinnae ken," Barn said. "Though I've been in the States for a long time, where I come from, once a man meets a woman, he takes her for his wife. There's none of this dilly-dallying with other lassies."

That was assuring.

I chewed on my lip, debating how much to divulge about Malton's possible role in Woody's death. Getting no indication Barn knew about Malton's cagey conduct in the park, I plunged on. "Were you aware of Malton's bitterness toward Woody?"

He spread his hands wide on the counter, a man bracing himself for the worst. "Explain yourself, lass."

I gulped down a breath, not wanting to instill negative thoughts in Barn's head. It was clear he saw the best in people, but what did he really know about his clanmates? "Seems Woody had, uh, dilly-dallied with Malton's girlfriend."

He met my gaze with dismay, then puffed out a

mouthful of air. "Wouldn't surprise me. The lad couldn't keep it in his pants."

"For some, that'd be a good motive for murder."

He squinted one eye shut. "I see where you're going with this."

My thoughts wandered back to yesterday's threat from Malton and last night's incident at the outhouse. Even if Malton hadn't been the one who'd locked me in, his actions earlier had been deplorable. There was no way to buffer my next question, but it needed to be asked. "Have you ever known Malton to physically hurt someone?"

He blinked in surprise, his accent robust. "MacGregor?"

"Yes. I know about his criminal record. And there's an air to him that's unnerving."

"Aye, he's a wild one and difficult to rein in, but I doubt he'd be so mean as to physically hurt another person."

Someone had to rip off Barn's rose-colored glasses. "What about locking someone in a porta potty? Think he's capable of *that*?" I stretched my neck up at him, raising my eyebrow for good measure.

He gave a hearty chuckle at my pluck. "*That* I could see. But I'm sure it'd be done in good fun."

Mmm. Loads of fun.

I wanted to ask about Hoagy's hostility toward Malton, but since Malton boinking Hoagy's girlfriend didn't directly relate to the case, it seemed unwarranted.

Barn smiled at someone over my shoulder and gave a friendly wave. "Imagine the fun you'd have in a silly disguise like that mascot." He chuckled. "You could get away with bloody murder."

"Huh?" I swiveled around, tripped on my skirt, and went down hard. Before my hands hit the ground, I spied the globe six feet away, prancing backward, giving me a little finger wave. I squealed in shock, and Barn rushed out to help me.

He scooped me in his arms and held me to his mammoth chest. "You okay, lass?"

I scarcely heard his words for the ton of bricks hitting me from his "bloody murder" remark.

He was right. Who else could get away with murder and sneak around the park undetected in plain sight other than someone in full body disguise? The mascot fit the bill perfectly. How could I've missed it?

Suddenly, I recalled Tantig's story about spotting the mascot Friday night around the porta potties. Come to think of it, it had also been loitering in the field yesterday when Max and I'd been talking to Romero about the homicide. Then there'd been my walk to the car last night when it had startled me. Three strange sightings. It had been under my nose the entire time. I just hadn't connected the dots.

Trying to keep track of its whereabouts, I struggled to free myself from Barn's embrace, swinging my arms and legs like an octopus, cranking my head this way and that. The crowd had thickened as morning turned into noon, and pegging anything more than a few feet away proved futile. *Darn.* Where'd it go?

I scanned the area while more pieces fell into place. Specifically, the fuzzy image I'd noticed late last night when I'd returned to the park. It had to have been the globe. If the disguised killer had overheard Romero telling me about the concealed weapon, chances were he'd become nervous about where he'd hidden the evidence. Maybe he'd figured on waiting until the park closed to grab the paddle and stash it somewhere else, even clean off the blood.

The conversation I'd had with Emery popped to mind and triggered what had brought on the earlier unease. He'd mentioned that a small person had to be inside the globe. Someone who'd been bullied. Not really a kid. Just another fair worker. A *female* fair worker.

A shiver darted up my spine while pins of anxiety stabbed my chest. *Adia.* She was that fair worker! Not only was she small, but she could've been bullied because of her heritage. *Welcome to the club.* Was that in fact what

Max had alluded to when he'd said that Adia had appeared different than anyone he'd ever met? Had they become fast friends because they'd both experienced singling out?

Deflated, I slumped in Barn's arms, my one shoe falling to the ground. "I'm fine. Thank you."

"You sure?" He bent forward and gently placed me on my feet. "You went down like you'd been slammed in a wrestling match."

Right. A regular day at the WWE. "I'm sure. But I've got to run." I reached for my bag, slipped halfway into my loafer, and hopped away, catching his shout in the background to be careful.

With everything I'd learned over the weekend about Adia, from her unstable relationship with Woody, to the notes that she'd undoubtedly written, to her admission to Malton that she was glad Woody was dead, to her whereabouts when Max had planned to meet her, to this latest discovery about the disguise, she *had* to have been the murderer! She had the perfect motive, and she had opportunity.

Her need to return to the hidden paddle last night also explained why her date with Max had been cut short. It also told me who'd pushed me into the outhouse.

I sprinted fifty yards in the direction I'd last seen the globe. Not spying it anywhere, I stopped to catch my breath and readjusted my shoe. "Where are you?" I muttered, looking behind me in case it had circled back.

Adia was damn clever. Dressed as the mascot, she could've kept her eye on the entire investigation. Was it also possible she'd decided to taunt me because she'd been envious of my relationship with Max? Seemed absurd, but if she had a jealous streak, it was conceivable this trait could've extended into other areas of her life. Yet surely Emery would've mentioned Adia as the person parading around in the globe. If he knew it'd been her. After all, he'd seen her and Woody arguing. Therefore, he'd been familiar with her looks.

But hold on. Emery never mentioned that he knew the mascot's identity. It was possible he only saw the person in disguise like the rest of us. And as affable as Emery was, he simply could've reached out to a new pal in the park who happened to be dressed as a globe.

I swallowed a hard gulp. What would've happened last night if Jock hadn't shown up at the outhouse when he did? His presence had likely scared off Adia before she could strike again.

I continued to search the grounds, but a needling feeling alerted me that something was off about the mascot. I couldn't pinpoint what it was, yet I'd sensed it when it had waved to me. It was dressed as it always had been. Same height. Same width. Big goofy white gloves. Padded feet. Nothing different there.

I stood rooted in the middle of traffic, getting jostled this way and that while I combed my thoughts as to what was altered.

"Oops, sorry, Miss." A guy reached for my elbow after bumping into me. "Shouldn't have been looking down at this little doohickey."

He pulled at his collar, displaying a two-inch replica of the globe mascot. On its round head was a gemmed French beret with hair strands sticking out all over. "There's a guy selling all kinds of these handmade pins with hats of every country glued to their heads. He calls them his 'Get Out of Town' world collection." He laughed and petted his globe. "This one's 'Get Out of Town Paree.' Ever hear of anything so crazy?"

I smiled politely. "Believe it or not…yes."

He smiled back in awe. "Only in America."

He went on his way and I frowned, returning to what was off about the real globe. I stared from the guy's back to the ground to where the mascot had disappeared. Dang. What was it that was different?

I pivoted back to the guy, recalling how taken he'd been with his doohickey. Friendly enough, even if he'd been focused on Kashi's brooch. That was it! He was wearing one of Kashi's brooches. And so was the globe! Only the globe's brooch wasn't sporting a French beret. It was modeling a red plaid Scottish tam.

If Adia was inside that globe, was this her way of thumbing her nose at Woody, a Scotsman who'd been a lying cheat? Her way of saying *Good riddance, you snake in the grass?*

I didn't think the mascot had been wearing a "Get Out of Town" brooch earlier, and I knew for certain it hadn't been wearing one yesterday—and we'd seen each other more than a few times during the day. I picked up my skirt and hurried past festivalgoers to Kashi's tent. He'd tell me who'd purchased the brooch.

Instantly, my thoughts veered back to my tiff with Max, and I stumbled out of sheer misery. *Jeepers.* Bad enough we were barely on speaking terms, but this strain on our friendship was eating me up inside. What would happen in the next few minutes when I entered the Indian tent? Would he be mad at seeing me, figuring I was there to instill more harm? My feet weighed down like lead at the prospect, Max's wounded face more than I could handle.

I could avoid seeing him altogether and slip through Kashi's front entrance instead of Pandi's, but I needed to know if he was still filling in for Adia. Essentially, it wouldn't matter what I said to Max. He'd look at me with suspicious eyes until he was good and ready to let go of this grudge.

Thing was, if Adia was back, that would tell me she couldn't possibly have been the mascot, proving a number of my other theories wrong. If that happened, I'd squeal with delight and make everything better with Max.

I stopped walking and found myself in front of Pandi's tent. It was now or never. I took a huge breath, asked God to please have Adia be inside the tent, and plowed through the opening.

No luck. Max stood behind the counter, bagging an item for a customer, a smile in place. Even with the smile, there was a shadow of concern in his eyes. He spotted me fidgeting near the entrance and knit his eyebrows together. Curious...or else mad, like I figured.

Did I use this opportunity to tell him Romero had rushed off to Gupta's Getaways? That there'd been a new development in the case? It didn't mean Pandi was off the hook, and potentially it could be worse news.

Max had a line of people waiting to purchase things. I didn't want to hold him up, but I had to find out if Adia had returned. She could've been in the back room for all I knew.

I gained some courage, sidled up to the counter, and attempted to sound carefree. "You still filling in for Adia?"

"Yes." No preamble here.

My stomach churned with a mix of dread and fear, and I wanted to scream *No, tell me she's here*! But I knew Max was telling the truth. Just as I knew Adia was inside that globe. No matter what Romero learned, that didn't change this. It was her taunting me while Max slaved away in her tent.

A short, stout woman trundled up to the counter next with a long, flowing sari in her arms. She gave a timid look from Max to me like she didn't want to interrupt anything. My heart was bleeding for what Max would soon learn, and I could feel tears threatening to surface. But I fought for control and gave the woman a valiant smile. She smiled back meaningfully. She *had* interrupted something. Without offering a word, she quietly spread the sari on the counter.

That was it, then. I gave Max a dull wave, wanting to say more, but what was there to say? He'd made his decision. I'd made mine. In fact, I was beginning to regret the things I *had* said. All that baloney about taking sides and digging for more clues.

I huffed out air, infuriated and at my limit. If truth be told, I *was* taking sides. The side of the law. Sure, I'd keep digging for clues, and I'd dig till the bitter end. But if those clues nailed Adia to the cross, then God save her because she was going to need divine help.

If Max wanted to go down with Adia, then I had to face reality and say goodbye to one of the best friends I'd ever had. I loved Max, but I wouldn't stand around and watch him ruin his life. I couldn't do it. I had to do what my conscience allowed and pray one day he'd see I was doing this for him. It didn't seem that way now. But maybe one day.

There was a weak hollow at the base of my throat and a hole in my gut the size of a crater. Neither of which could be easily fixed, but I steamrollered on, ruthless to the core. I was going to catch a murderer. I had to.

I turned my back on Max, cleared a path to Kashi's tent, and ripped back the flap.

"*Aaah!*" Kashi screamed at my entrance.

I couldn't blame him. Not only was I dressed in red, but no doubt there was fire in my eyes and steam piping out my ears.

Two women who'd been admiring Kashi's brooches looked up in alarm. They dropped the pins on the counter with a clatter, stuffed their purses under their arms, and scrambled out of the tent.

Kashi drew his fists under his chin. "Am I in trouble? Are you here to beat me to a paste?"

"That's *pulp*!" I cried, sick of correcting Kashi's faux pas. I stomped over to his counter, my bag swinging from my arm like Rambo's machine gun.

He backed up a foot, hands high. "I swear, I have done nothing!"

I slapped my palms on the glass top, my frame of mind worsening by the minute. "Where is it?"

"*Here. Take it.*" He slid his cash box to me. "It's only money."

"I don't want your money."

He shifted his eyes from side to side, like was this a prank? "Then what do you want?"

I examined his tent, housing all his brooches, then focused on the display case in front of me. "Your 'Get Out of Town' world collection."

He blinked, confused. "You want to see my world collection? Why didn't you say so?"

He stepped behind a second counter and gestured at hundreds of tiny mascots. Some had cowboy hats, others had Mexican sombreros. All had Kashi's signature hair and gems poking out every which way. If I hadn't been acting like a raving psycho, I would've admitted the furry things were darn cute.

I calmed myself and took a moment to mentally phrase my question. This was too important to be misconstrued. "Kashi, I need to know who bought the mascot with the Scottish tam."

He pulled out two wearing tams. "With a blue tam or red?" He plucked out a third. "Or green?"

"Red," I barked.

He flinched, and the brooches slipped to the counter with a clink. "I don't know! They're my biggest seller. Everyone wants a Kashi 'Get Out of Town Scotty'."

This was getting me nowhere. I needed to come at it from another angle. "Okay, Kashi. Did the big globe mascot come in to buy one of the brooches?"

He frowned like he didn't understand the question. "You mean, did I sell a 'Get Out of Town' brooch to the real mascot?"

"Yes, the real mascot. Not just any brooch, though. Your 'Get Out of Town Scotty'." Before he asked which color, I added, "With the red tam."

"Ohhh." He straightened, breathing with ease. "No."

"*NO?*"

"*Aaah!*" He leaped a foot in the air. "Yes?"

"Kashi, which is it?"

"What do you want it to be?"

I whacked my hands to my head, sure I was going to combust. The day was marching on, and I didn't have precious time to play Abbott and Costello with him.

Taking things down a notch, I lowered my hands and shifted my bag over my shoulder. "Kashi, I want you to think hard. Did the globe come in here at *any time* this weekend and buy one of your brooches?"

"What are you going to do if I say no again?"

"Nothing."

He took a step back, guarding his chest with his hands. "No."

I blew out in exasperation. Now for the tough question. "What about Adia? Did she buy a brooch from you?"

He put his shaky finger under his chin, aiming it next door. "Pandi's daughter, Adia?"

"Yes, that Adia."

He pushed his glasses up his nose, his eyes wide. "Why are you asking about her?"

Kashi apparently hadn't been privy to unfolding events since Woody's murder. And I was in such a hurry to catch the killer, I didn't want to waste a minute connecting the dots for him. Instead, I fired more questions, not giving him time to think.

"Since you knew Pandi through sports, did you know his cricket paddle was found with blood on it?"

His eyebrows went up, and his glasses slid down. "No."

"Did you know anything about Pandi's partnership with Woody?"

"No!"

"Did you know Pandi could be involved in murder?"

"*No!*"

I took a deep breath. "This is why I'm asking about Adia. Now, did she buy a brooch from you or not?"

"Yes."

"*Yes?*"

"That is what I said."

"Was it the 'Get Out of Town Scotty'?"

Kashi looked like he was about to pee his pants, not sure which answer I wanted. "I can't remember. I have sold so many this weekend, I can't keep track."

I clunked my silver wristband on the counter, at my wit's end.

"Wait!" he cried. "Yes, I do remember. Adia did buy my 'Get Out of Town Scotty' yesterday. She said it was in honor of Woody's death."

That was the last clue I needed to prove that Adia was the murderer and inside that costume. I yelled a thanks to Kashi over my shoulder and dove out of the tent.

Chapter 17

I had no idea where I was running, but I had to find Adia. Perhaps there was nothing left to salvage in my relationship with Max, but if her friendship was what he wanted, maybe I'd convince her to give herself up. If she really cared for Max, she'd do the right thing.

I bumped into people left and right, blindly pushing my way through the crowd. My heart was thrashing violently inside my rib cage, and nausea was building in the pit of my gut. It was just a matter of time before I found Adia. But what would I say when I did?

I ran the entire area twice and didn't spot the globe anywhere. Only happy people, enjoying the festivities. I keeled forward, panting for air, seeing double from sweat dripping in my eyes. Holding my side, I hobbled over to a bench and flopped down, bag to the ground, arms on my knees. *Holy Moses.* I needed a better fitness regime. Zumba obviously wasn't cutting it.

Forgetting my issues, I wiped the sweat from my eyes and asked myself where the globe would hide. I was counting on seeing it out in the open, but what if it was taking shelter somewhere? Perhaps in one of the tents? A porta potty? No, nix that. It wouldn't fit in a porta potty.

I took a gulp of water from a nearby fountain and was fanning my face when I caught sight of a big blue and green blob. The globe! And it was heading for the midway.

I swiped my bag off the ground, bulldozed through the crowd, and raced in the same direction.

Sensing it was being chased, the globe turned sideways and spotted me, a blur of red, coming after it like a ball of fire. In a fit of panic, as if suddenly realizing I'd pegged it as the murderer, it flapped its arms in the air, jackknifed its knees high, and detoured for the Ferris wheel.

"Aha!" I shouted. "Gotcha now!"

Sure. Not only did I *not* have the globe, if I ever caught up to it, how would I seize it?

The Ferris wheel slowed to a stop to take on riders. The mascot barreled through the line and climbed onto a bench before anyone else.

"Wait!" I squawked, as the operator advanced it to the next level.

Unaware of the commotion, a man climbed on first, sat down, and went for the safety harness. I elbowed him aside and plopped on the seat next to him.

"Hey!" he cried. "My wife was going to sit there."

"She'll have to wait her turn." I pretended to lock myself in until we were moving. Then I flung the harness back, stood up on the seat, and stretched for the carriage over us.

"What are you doing?" The guy held onto the bars at the side, steadying our car.

"I need to get to that mascot."

He looked up at the globe, then back at me like he was wondering if I were for real. Then he glanced down at the ground, which was getting further away by the second. "Lady, sit down! We're going higher!"

I didn't care if we were soaring to the moon. I wasn't stopping until I had my hands on that globe. I swept my skirt between my legs, hiked it up to my crotch, and tied the ends in a knot. Our car swung dangerously under my jiggling, and a screw popped from the ceiling to the floor.

The guy's mouth dropped open at the screw, and a bead of sweat sprang to his lip. The screw rotated in a circle, then rolled to the edge, and fell off the side. The man stretched his neck beyond the safety of the car and followed the screw's descent. Then he raised his head and looked around, unable to find words. I wanted to tell him better days were ahead, but at this rate, I wasn't sure we'd survive the next hour.

The carriage continued to sway back and forth, threatening to tip us thirty feet to the ground. Swallowing that fear, I hooked my bag over my back, secured my hands on the bars by my head, and stepped on his lap to set myself higher.

"Owww!" He squirmed under my weight. "Do you have to use *me* as a footstool?"

I peered under my armpit at him, not appreciating his resistance one bit. I was laying my life on the line for Max, for this park, for the good of Rueland. Even for *him*. In addition, I couldn't stop shaking for the panic blasting me. But I wasn't giving up now. Too much depended on this.

I hopped back down with clenched teeth, wrapped my fingers around the guy's ears, and yanked him nose to nose. "Listen, Mack. You have two choices. You can either help me catch a killer, or you can sit quietly with your head up your ass. Either way, I'm going up there."

I wasn't proud of my aggression, but someone had to set the guy straight.

He nodded his head up and down like a bobblehead, probably thinking it wiser to cooperate with a visibly unstable person.

I climbed back onto the seat and stepped on his lap again. Without a word, he boosted me up. I reached for the next rung and set my feet on his shoulders. Then I hauled myself higher to the bottom of the globe's carriage above.

The big ball squirmed and hung onto the sides for dear life, hastily stamping the cage floor in hopes of scaring me off. Ha! Good luck with that. I had more crucial things to worry about than a sicko's dancing feet.

Concentrating on my actions, I employed one of my

old ballet steps and balanced myself between the moving mechanisms. Then I tore my bag around to my front and rifled through it. I glanced up at the globe eight feet away, then back at my bag. *Come on. Come on. Come on.* What did I have that would bring this girl down? Without dwelling on my lack of real weapons, I pulled out a bottle of perm solution, gave it a good shake, and split open the nozzle with my teeth.

Suddenly, the Ferris wheel gave an alarming lurch. Riders screeched from their cars, and I gasped, suppressing the instant drop in my stomach. Time stood still, the tension terrifying from up here. *Focus, Valentine. Don't think about being two hundred feet in the air. Just don't look down.* I froze, breathing shallow breaths, when finally the Ferris wheel picked up again. The new jolt caused me to lose my footing, and I slipped forward and bounced halfway over the rail.

"*Aaaaah!*"

I flailed my arm for something to grab, horror streaming through my veins. I accidentally knuckled the bar by my head, then clutched it and pulled back in time before I plummeted to my death.

My heart stopped cold, and I lost track of my breathing. I tried to expand my lungs, in and out, but I was powerless to move, unable to calm down.

People were shrieking below, and out of the corner of my eye, I saw the crowd growing.

"Don't jump!" someone shouted.

Jump? Good one.

My clothes were drenched with sweat, and I was dizzy from shock. With only one hand on the bar, I was losing my grasp.

"You gotta grip that steel rod by your leg," Mack said, "then slip yourself down till you're standing on the carriage's frame."

By now, we'd escalated to the highest point and were on the return trip down. This meant I was currently on top of the mascot. It pointed its goofy glove at me, its

"Get Out of Town Scotty" taunting me from its big round chest.

"Hey, you moron!" a person from the next car yelled to Mack. "You have a death wish for us all? She's so crazy she's going to tip this whole Ferris wheel over."

"Sorry," Mack said with a shrug.

I pulled myself together and did what Mack suggested. Then I remembered the bottle of perm solution in my hand. I loosened my death grip on the bottle and aimed it down at the globe's mouth, squeezing for all I was worth. My hope was that it'd seep through the material and douse Adia's face. I didn't want to mar or blind her, and I wasn't sure what damage ammonium thioglycolate would do. But I had to try something that would weaken her ability when we got to the ground.

Within seconds, I heard sputtering and coughing from inside the globe. Its big white hands shot down in pain. Once its carriage reached the ground, it took off as fast as its large feet would carry it.

I hit the platform a moment later and ran twenty paces after the mascot, but my legs gave out, and I collapsed to the ground, shaking and sobbing frightened tears that finally gave way.

"You can't quit now!" Mack scooped me up from behind and snatched the empty bottle. "You didn't put us through hell back there for nothing." He shoved my butt. "Now go!"

I teared up more because of his support. But he was right. I'd come this far. I had to stop that globe. I swiped away tears with my fist, inhaled a gulp of air, and prayed for strength and courage. People darted out of the way as I rushed by, not sure who to help. That was fine because I was gaining on our shady mascot, at an advantage since I was in loafers and it was in huge, stuffed shoes.

It headed for the pond, picking up speed like it knew this was a matter of life and death. It twisted around to see how close I was getting, then lost momentum and toppled to the ground. I crashed into it, sank my fingers into its padding, and we rolled down a slope, landing eight feet from the water's edge. Grass and mud stuck to us while moisture from the damp ground saturated my pores.

Fear seized me inside, the dizziness from earlier escalating to lightheadedness. I shook my head to dispel the faintness and wrestled to gain my footing. My bag! Where was my bag? Forcing myself to get control, I clambered to my feet to scope the area but fell back down, my balance unsteady.

The mob had dispersed when we'd veered from the midway, reality hitting me that I was on my own. Spurred on by our seclusion, the globe bounced to its feet and stumbled toward me. Something about its determination told me I was going to lose this battle, but woozy as I was, I wasn't giving up without a fight.

It pounced on me, straining to secure my arms. I flailed and kicked for all I was worth, loosening its "Get Out of Town Scotty" from its chest. I scrabbled the ground with my hands, swinging my head back and forth, hoping to grip my bag. But it was too far away, its contents strewn everywhere.

Screaming in terror, I wriggled viciously, throwing handfuls of dirt. Then I fingered something skinny like a twig. I clasped it tightly just as the globe swooped me up and carried me to the water. Powerful little wench! But this whacko wasn't going to beat me.

"Put me *down*!" I thrashed around on its back, recognizing the twig in my hand was nothing but a metal crochet hook. I'd once used it to pull hair through a streaking cap when I ran out of foil for highlighting. Why I still carted it in my bag was anyone's guess. *Who cares! Use it!*

Striving for might, I punctured the tool through the globe's cushioning, getting muffled *eeks* and *owws*. No collapsing. No surrendering. What was I thinking? I wasn't going to bring down this rotund ball with a measly crochet hook.

The globe flipped me into the pond, the algae-infested cold water stunning my skin. I shook off the shock, and we sloshed around in hip-deep swamp for what seemed like an eternity. My foe smacked me with its hefty gloves, and I speared it anywhere I could.

Having enough of this, it lunged for me in an all-or-nothing charge. "Take your last breath," it whispered its first words. And, I was afraid, the last words I'd ever hear.

It held me down in the water, crushing me with significant force. Holding in air, I used what little strength I had left, stabbing violently at its legs. It lost its footing, attempting to escape my pricks, but I was on a mission.

In the span of two days, I'd been sucked into another murder case, had all but lost my best friend, been humiliated, scared, and attacked in too many ways to count. I wasn't going to be overthrown by a crazy chick in a dumb, world getup.

I sputtered to the surface, gagging and coughing, a powerful will to survive overcoming me. In a massive show of effort, I rose out of the water, stretched my arms like the Hulk, and with a gut-wrenching cry, came down hard with a final jab on the globe. For Woody and all the victims who'd been silenced before their time, this was for them.

Blood colored the water, and the globe flopped on its back in agony.

I let out a sigh in victory and bent forward, struggling to right my breathing. Physically and mentally exhausted, I trudged over to the globe and reached a clammy hand for the Velcro strip by its head. If nothing else, I had to see Adia face to face.

I gripped the Velcro, and before I could rip it off, the globe flung its arm out of the water and brutally backhanded me across the head. The crochet hook sailed through the air, and I momentarily saw stars as I fell back into the pond.

Dazed and spent, I couldn't get my footing fast enough. The globe lunged for my neck and plunged me deeper into the water, sucking the air out of me.

I gasped and choked, swinging my arms like a lunatic, but I couldn't grasp anything on its big round body. I fell into oblivion, a sudden vision of Yitts's morning nudges blurring my thoughts. *Nooooo.* My throat ached in pain, my heart seized in sorrow. Who'd look after Yitts if I died? Who'd love her like I did? More images rushed to mind, hysterical sobs quaking my body.

The cold, numbing water washed away my tears and gurgled through my lungs, fading my memories of Yitts. My life was about to end in my favorite park. One that had always been good to me. I sank deeper and deeper, losing consciousness, when I was forcefully released from the stronghold and thrust from the water.

In one swift move, I was tossed to the ground, wheezing and panting. I scrambled away for safety, covered in seaweed, sputtering, retching to clear my lungs. My brain hadn't yet registered what was happening, but one thing I knew: I was alive.

The globe staggered out of the water moments later, hands up in front of whoever had helped me. It was swathed in pond scum and smudged in blood, its blue tights shredded, its "Get Out of Town Scotty" hanging by a thread. It was only when the globe was forced to the ground that I saw my soaking wet and limping hero was Max.

My head was aching from the punch I'd taken, and I was sitting in a puddle of water, blubbering in fits and starts. But through my falling tears, I thought Max had never looked more handsome. Having taken a beating himself, he sagged, cut and bruised, to his knees.

I hung my head and squeezed my eyes tight, thanking God for Max, though I wasn't sure where things stood or if we'd ever talk again. Nonetheless, I had to reveal the murderer and put an end to this nightmare.

I grappled for a breath that all would be fine. Then I sniffed back tears and crawled on all fours to the globe. It was sprawled out, face up, limbs wide. Motionless. Defeated.

I placed my trembling hands on the Velcro strip, closed my eyes, head tilted back in silent prayer. Then I ripped off the lid.

"Emery!" I jumped back in shock, coughing from ammonia fumes escaping the inside of his costume. Startled yet relieved it wasn't Adia, I wanted to run over and hug Max. But he was gone. I turned my head left and right. No Max anywhere.

Emery gulped in fresh air and scrambled back in a crab-walk. "Stay away from me! You unhinged, psychotic, sadistic broad!"

Amazing how his golly-gee manner had disappeared. "You forgot nutty as a fruitcake." I inched closer, not sure where the sudden bravery had come from.

"Stay there!" He lost his balance, and his large, stout form plopped to the ground.

His clumsiness brought to mind the episode with the globe last night on my way to the parking lot. It had tripped over its padded feet after it had scared me. And earlier, it had stumbled while eavesdropping on Romero, Max, and me. So Emery had been in that costume, not Adia. Then there was Jock's story of the spilled paint at Gupta's Getaways. I'd even witnessed Emery this morning drop his phone to the ground when he went to slide it in his pocket.

Why hadn't I picked up on his ungainliness before and matched it to the globe? The easy answer was the fact that I'd been so set on Adia being the killer, I hadn't once stopped to notice how awkward the mascot truly was or pair it to Emery.

Emery's face was blotched from the perm solution, his scalp was covered in gouges, and his legs were leaking blood. "I think you punctured an artery. Look at me. I'm gushing like a sprinkler!"

"Don't be ridiculous. A sprinkler has bigger holes." I summed up his injuries. "And I didn't puncture an artery."

He gaped from his legs to me. "Oh. You some kind of expert on how deep a wound can be before it's fatal?"

"They're just nicks. You'll live."

"*Nicks.*" He struggled to a sitting position. "It felt like you were doing acupuncture. I have a right to know what you stabbed me with."

"A crochet hook. Happy?"

He narrowed his eyes to slits. "What's a beautician doing carrying a crochet hook?"

I wasn't about to give him a rundown on the tools I carried. I dashed over to my bag and scraped up cotton balls strewn on the ground beside it. I hustled back, dropped the cotton balls next to us, and went to work plugging holes.

"What are you doing?"

"You want to stop the bleeding, don't you?"

He picked a cotton ball off the ground with his gloved hand. "These have dirt on them. That's not hygienic. I could get an infection."

I leaned back on my knees. "You want to bleed to death?"

"A second ago you said I wasn't going to die."

I heaved out a breath, then swung my knees out from under me and plunked down beside him, giving us both a moment to get a grip.

Amid the silence surrounding us, he stuck the cotton ball to a gash. "This is downright embarrassing. What am I supposed to tell people when they ask what happened?"

"Tell them you're getting over the chickenpox."

"That'd be lying. I'm ashamed you even suggested it."

Oh boy. "I don't care what you tell them, Emery. I want to know why you did it."

He put his head down, sighing like he'd finally given up. "He threatened me."

"Woody?"

"Who else?" he snapped. "I'd set up their computer program at the hotel like I'd told you, and Woody caught me scamming from their site. Told me I had 24 hours to give all those innocent people back their money, or he'd report me to the police."

"When was that?"

"Thursday night," he said. "Day before we set up for the fair."

Somewhere in the back of my mind, I remembered Romero saying he was working on a cybercrime case involving someone swindling old ladies out of their grocery money. Had he figured Emery as the scammer? Was this the break he'd referred to?

And what about the Cutlers? It was clear they'd been fed a line about their friend's menial desk job. I just hoped they hadn't been cheated.

"So you killed Woody."

Emery held out his arm for me to take off his glove. "I couldn't let him go to the *police*. I was too far in. I had people to answer to."

I unsnapped his glove from his wrist and handed it to him, simultaneously tracing back to the events leading up to Woody's death. Particularly, Woody helping Tantig into the outhouse. "That was you arguing with Woody at the porta potties." I recalled Tantig saying Woody's ring glowed red. Apparently the result of the argument with Emery.

"That's right." Struggling to reach over his width, he yanked off his other glove and set them both on the ground. "I still had time to beg him not to report me. Woody had been busy anyway with his new venture with Pandi. I didn't think he'd given it much thought. But I couldn't take a chance. I asked him one last time not to go to the police. That's when that old lady came up to use the latrine. Good thing I'd given my costume a test run Friday night. She didn't seem to give me a second glance."

The costume. Of course. Didn't Tantig say she couldn't decipher who'd been talking to Woody because the voice had been too muffled to tell?

"Still," Emery went on, "I made myself scarce and hid behind the units until she went inside, then told Woody to meet me by the pond after setup closed for the night. I had an offer he couldn't refuse."

I scooped up the rest of the cotton balls and held them out in my palm. "But rather than make an offer, you stole Pandi's cricket paddle, waited for Woody at the pond, then clunked him on the head and killed him."

He took a cotton ball from my hand and dabbed another gash. "Everyone thinks I'm just some dumb oaf, but it takes a lot of brains to plan what I did. Not to mention strength." He became hoarse, and a tear popped out on his lower lid. "Short people have muscle, too, you know."

"Yes, I know." The tear struck a chord inside. Had Emery been referring to himself this morning when he'd said a fair worker couldn't be bullied in a costume?

Festivalgoers slowly appeared, hedging the international flags that flapped high over the area. Still no sign of Max.

Easing my shoulders, I came back to Emery. "You couldn't have been dressed as the mascot the entire time this weekend. I bumped into the globe yesterday when I first met you talking with the Cutlers. And this morning I came up to you and the globe at the midway."

His glare was cold. "We had our shifts, okay? Mine started yesterday at 3:30 *after* I'd met you."

My head was still groggy from the blow, but it all made sense. If he'd suited up at 3:30, it had also been him keeping tabs on me when I'd been on my way to quiz Barn and the other Scots.

"Every time I turned around, you were grilling someone. You know you're a pain in the buttocks? I should've nailed shut that porta potty door last night when I had the chance."

I spied him out of the corner of my eye. "So it was you."

"Who else?" He reached over his costumed belly and squeezed his legs in agony. "When's help going to get here? I think I need a doctor."

I blew out in a huff. "Boy, you're a moaner. You'd think you were stabbed in the chest."

He looked indignant. "Easy for you to say. You were the one with the crochet hook."

"And *you* punched me in the *head*."

"What would *you* do if someone was poking you like a pincushion?"

I jammed another cotton ball on his leg with little care. "Could we finish the explanations before you go into cardiac arrest?"

He folded his arms across his chest. "You know, you're not too genial. There's not one ounce of sympathy in your voice. I wouldn't be surprised if they locked *you* up."

I cut him a caustic glance. "Until they do, answer this. If you were the globe only part of the time, who dressed for the other part?"

"It was one of the fair workers from the Spanish tent, all right? She happened to be the right size, and she wanted to help."

"So it wasn't Adia." I had to be clear.

He gave me a scornful look. "Why would Adia dress up as a dumb globe?"

Good point.

Sirens wailed in the distance, and the crowd leaped out of the way as Romero barreled through, a squad of uniforms behind him. His hair was wild, his manner tense. No question, Romero was in dangerous-cop mode, and he meant business.

Max was a step behind, a look of triumph on his bruised face. Even from a distance, I could see his sincere smile directed at me, a smile that released the wounds around my heart. I swallowed with sudden tears and nodded back, our eye contact one that couldn't be measured with words yet was full of meaning.

Emery stretched his neck to see what the fuss was about. After spotting Romero and the descending uniforms, he rolled his eyes to the top of his head and slumped to the ground.

I considered doing the same thing. Preservation, I told myself. No telling what Romero would do because I hadn't heeded his warning earlier to stay out of trouble.

The cops pulled Emery to his feet, and Romero jogged

over to me. He held out his hand, helped me up, and studied me from head to toe. I could imagine what he was thinking. My hat was askew, my skirt was in shreds, and gunk was smeared everywhere. *And* I smelled like swamp water. If we hadn't been surrounded by a ton of people and the situation hadn't been so dire, he might've cracked a smile. All I got were blackening eyes like the night, searing through me, and a twitching vein in his neck that may have been blood pressure-related. "You have a lot of explaining to do. You realize you almost got yourself kil—"

I raised my pointer finger before he blew, signaling him to hold on a minute. Imagine that. Me advising Romero to hold on. Not that I was trying to evade the coming lecture, but a squishy sensation in my shoe was pulling my attention.

Romero dropped his jaw in surprise, his opportunity to holler snatched away. Recuperating quickly, he folded his arms in front and tightened his lips, his reddening face the shade of my ripped skirt. I was acquainted with this look, and it wasn't his happy face.

Ignoring that for more important things, I clutched his arm for support, bent over, and removed my loafer. I tipped it upside down, and a minnow flopped to the ground. Looking stunned, it wiggled its silvery body toward the pond in an effort to get home. Poor thing.

I pinched it by the tail and tossed it back in the water, distinctly feeling Romero's eyes blazing through me. I peered up at him with an innocent smile. "You can't stay mad at someone who just saved a life."

Chapter 18

The multicultural fair disbanded for another year, and the rest of the week went by in a flurry. The murderer had been placed under arrest, and Rueland's city council was taking steps to ensure everyone's safety at not just the town park but every recreational area in Rueland.

Emotionally, it'd take a while to bury the harsh memories from the fair and get over the fact that I, too, had almost lost my life in the same pond as Woody. At the hands of a globetrotting mascot, yet. But the marks would heal, and I'd become stronger. So what if I never looked at a mascot the same way again. My faith had been restored in the peace and tranquility of my special childhood place, and all those times I'd spent in the park would forever be cherished.

By Saturday, things had returned to normal at the salon. Phyllis had made short work of the donuts Friar Tuck's had bequeathed her, and after another bout of indigestion, she went on a sugar fast. My mother had given her the leftover tabbouleh from the fair and encouraged her to try a Mediterranean diet. Phyllis was hooked and was currently in talks at Friar Tuck's, thinking they'd jump at her suggestion to make tabbouleh donuts. Another disaster waiting to happen.

Phyllis had also made a small profit on her "Get the

Hell Out of Here" scarves from the fair and insisted on selling the remaining heap in the salon. If she sold one scarf per day, she wouldn't get rid of them until Christmas or make up the money she owed me for the Italian-made hair extensions. Was it any wonder I couldn't get ahead?

Jock had skipped out of work early to finish the stone entrance at Gupta's Getaways. I can say I was grateful for that. His intimate stares and innocent touches all week had made me hot and nearly orgasmic. Plus, he promised the next time he saw me in my *ballet* suit, he was going to insist I teach him lessons. Specifically, how to bend, stretch, and glide.

I coughed out a shaky *okey-dokey* at that, picturing myself bending or stretching anywhere near Jock. He wasn't only Hercules, Thor, and Superman wrapped into one; he possessed undeniable stamina when it came to poise and grace. If anyone taught anyone moves, it'd be *him* teaching *me*. But I wasn't going to point that out.

I'd set him straight where we were concerned, thinking my deepening relationship with Romero would keep him at bay, but Jock beat to a different drum. No doubt persistence had paid off before.

A strange feeling came over me as a new thought took hold, a thought I had to take time to reflect on. Jock would find somebody one day and turn his attention elsewhere.

Was that what I wanted? Another woman in Jock's life? Would that make things easier for me? What would that do to our work relationship? Our friendship? I swallowed, letting the thoughts drift from my mind. It wasn't something I wished to dwell on. One day maybe. But not today.

Max hugged his last client goodbye, and I swept the floor, watching him flex his back muscles in pain. His scrapes and bruises from his match with Emery had healed, and it hadn't appeared he'd suffered any traumatic injuries. If anything, there was a lighter bounce to his step.

He pivoted around on his heel and snapped his fingers.

"Another day, another dollar." He noticed the grin on my face, then narrowed his eyes. "*What?*"

I backed into the dispensary and swept the hair into the garbage. "Just feeling blessed by a certain Max Martell."

He cocked an eyebrow, waiting for an explanation.

"I didn't know you had it in you to physically fight off another human being." Max had come to my rescue before, but never had a confrontation involved hand-to-hand combat.

"Lovey," he began, his playful manner restored, "I'm not just handsome, talented, and clever. I'm the Terminator." He did a Mr. Universe pose, and I had to admit he had an impressive build. Maybe not to the extent of Arnold Schwarzenegger's Terminator, but impressive all the same.

"Anyway," he continued, "you did all the work seizing Emery. I simply finished up." He paused, his tone apologetic. "That's what friends do for one another."

I couldn't see straight for the tears filling my eyes. I turned to hide my emotions and dumped the dustpan and broom by the wall.

"And not that you've asked, but I want you to know that the friendship I had with Adia had its day twenty years ago. I thought we could build on that again, but to be honest, I didn't like who she'd become."

I straightened and blinked back the tears. "Really?"

Max had seemed taken by the beautiful girl, and I wasn't sure what the outcome of this case would do to him. Since Pandi had been released, Adia's relationship with Woody had made headlines. I couldn't see Max being too thrilled about Adia dating a womanizer or the fact that it had been in the news. But I had a feeling the tipping point was when Phyllis accidentally blurted she'd overheard Adia say she was glad Woody was dead.

Max gave a dismissive shrug. "Her superior attitude was tiring, and her jealousy over you got to me."

So she *had* resented me. It was still hard to fathom. "How could she be envious of me?"

"I know, right?"

I threw a pen from the counter at him, and the smartass caught it and slid it into his shirt pocket.

"She kept asking why I worked for you, and when was I going to open my own salon." He spread his arms wide. "This is my home, damn it! And you're my bestie, my pal, the other half of my ego. You know what I'm thinking before I even think it. What we have is mutual. She couldn't understand that." He exhaled, his attitude indifferent. "I wasn't into worshipping her, and I'd finally had enough of her badgering."

Max and I had faced a lot through the years. We didn't always agree on things, but I could always count on him to be truthful no matter how much it hurt. His confession boosted me to the inner core, and relief swam through my veins at such a rate I was almost giddy. "I'm glad you came to that decision on your own…hard as it might've been."

He grinned. "Miss Gypsy Rose Lee's revelation about what Adia had said didn't hurt. I couldn't be friends with someone who had such a hateful streak."

Kudos to Phyllis for spilling the beans. Somewhere in the depths of her soul I knew she loved Max. Maybe not like a brother or a bestie. Heck, probably not even like a pet dog. But she cared enough to tell Max what he needed to hear.

It'd been bothering me where Adia had gone when she'd asked Max to open her tent the last morning. Considering he was in a revealing mood, I pressed on with caution. "With Pandi in custody Sunday morning, I was curious…why'd you open for Adia?"

He nodded in understanding. "She had to go to the hotel and sort out urgent business."

I could appreciate that. Now that Woody was gone, Pandi would either need a new partner or go at it alone. I shrugged inside. Maybe Adia would step up and take on a role in her father's dynasty. "What about Saturday night?" Might as well get it all out on the table.

"Saturday night?"

"Yes. You were meeting her at the Ferris wheel, but she texted saying she forgot she had something to do, and she'd meet up at closing."

"Right. The Guptas were also helping run one of the other smaller tents. Adia was dashing in every direction, which, at first, was kind of admirable. But she got sour fast from everyone depending on her."

True, being depended on was a tall order, something I could relate to. But wasn't that part of life? Part of what made family? Community? It was nice to dream of being unencumbered, free of commitment, having no one need you. But that seemed a selfish existence, one that didn't appeal to me. "Was that also why the night was cut short?"

"Partly. She'd been worried about her dad and the business, and she wanted to make it an early night."

He stroked his chin, a thoughtful look in his eyes. "I'm glad Pandi was found innocent. I didn't want to see him go to jail for something he didn't do."

I agreed.

"And to be supportive, plus show there were no hard feelings, I bought a wooden elephant statue from Adia. Sort of as a memory of this whole affair. I'm going to call it Ellie."

I snickered at how alike we really were. "Sounds like the perfect name."

I'd had big plans for tonight, wanting to cook Romero a romantic ethnic dinner, and then…who knows? But the minute Emery was arrested, Romero had left with him for Baton Rouge. Seemed Emery was the missing link in the cybercrime double homicide investigation Romero had been involved in, and as Romero wanted to deliver Emery to the authorities himself, we were back to playing phone tag.

At least Romero had called from Baton Rouge and

cleared up the remaining questions I'd had about the case. Most notably, what Pandi's alibis had been for Friday, the night of the murder, and Saturday night when I'd been locked in the porta potty. It all seemed moot now since Emery had been placed under arrest, but curious minds and all that.

"Pandi practiced cricket with his team Friday night and made naan bread with the ladies Saturday evening," Romero said.

"Wait," I cut him off. "If Pandi's paddle was used to murder Woody Friday night, then what did he use to play cricket with?"

I could hear the smile in his voice. "Has anyone ever told you you're quick?"

"I am, aren't I?" I teased back.

"Here's the truth. Pandi couldn't find his bat Friday night to take to the practice at Watson Park. He thought he'd misplaced it with all the boxes and setup confusion. He wasn't worried because there were always extra bats on hand, and he figured his would pop up. Then he didn't think about it anymore until he was brought in and questioned."

I tapped my finger on the phone. "Then Pandi had no idea it had been stolen and used as the murder weapon."

"None at all," he confirmed.

"And Malton? I still had a feeling he'd been involved."

"Not directly. He'd beaten the shit out of Woody a few days prior to the festival, which accounted for the bruises on Woody's body—cleverly hidden where no one would see. Guess we couldn't give Emery all the credit for the marks."

Hmm. Maybe this was why Woody had trouble concentrating at soccer that Wednesday. He knew a fight with Malton was imminent for screwing around with his girlfriend. It also explained the argument Aileen had witnessed between the two that Friday night. Malton was probably still harassing Woody.

"What about the Cutlers?"

I detected a faint groan slip out. "Those British magpies?" During a past interrogation, Romero had threatened to handcuff the two chatterboxes if they didn't keep their groping hands to themselves. Naturally, nothing had excited them more.

"Yes, I mean, no." I grinned inside. "You know they're harmless, but they may have lost money due to Emery's scam."

"They were lucky. Emery's operation was headquartered in Boston and Baton Rouge. Rueland hadn't been affected yet, thanks to MacDunnell catching Emery when he did. MacDunnell may have died a womanizer, but he helped put the lid on this case." There was a moment's pause, and his cop voice softened. "As did you."

I beamed, not that he could see it. After promising he'd be back as soon as possible, he hung up.

To celebrate the closing of Woody's case, I treated myself to a pizza after work and a Friar Tuck's apple fritter. I ate half the pizza the minute I walked in the front door and savored the donut while I soaked in a hot tub bubbling with vanilla-scented foam bath. I'd put my hair up into a messy bun and munched away, listening to achy-breaky country music. Appropriate, since I was alone again on a Saturday night. But the sugar from the donut did miraculous things for my mood, and before I knew it, I was belting out the song's lyrics at the top of my lungs.

Yitts usually sat on the edge of the tub, pawing bubbles I blew at her. But recently she'd taken up nightly residency at Ellie's feet, finding comfort beneath her new friend. That was okay. I reflected on my earlier talk with Max. We all needed the luxury of a close pal.

I pulled the plug, dried off, and swathed myself with Musk lotion. *Ahh.* If there ever was a more beautiful scent, I hadn't found it. Feeling much better and more human than I'd felt in days, I slipped into my sheer baby-dolls and stepped into my puffy cupcake slippers. I wasn't tired and figured now was a good time to clean out my bag. Plus, it'd be good therapy.

After things were either pitched or Lysoled and put back, I tossed my bag by the piano and cleaned the rest of the house. No sense letting a fresh bowl of Lysol go to waste.

An hour later, I took a satisfying breath at everything looking neat and tidy, then settled in to watch a movie.

Hmm. What was I in the mood for? I flicked through old romantic comedies. On the heels of the past week's events, I needed a good laugh.

I had the lights down low but was wide-awake after Colin Firth kissed Renée Zellweger in *Bridget Jones's Diary*. Must've been all the sugar from the donut that was keeping me from dozing off. I sprang from the couch and did a jog on the spot. What to do? What to do? I had energy up the wazoo. Great. Now I sounded like Dr. Seuss.

I sprinted into the sparkling bathroom, brushed my teeth, and smacked my lips together. Yow. I was more wired than ever. I walked back into the living room, taking stock of things. I didn't feel like another movie. And the house was immaculate. Any more cleaning, and my hands would wither up. I mentally rolled back to last weekend, and in a flash I knew what to do.

I whizzed into my bedroom, pulled on yoga pants, and changed my pajama top for a sweatshirt that hung off the shoulders. Then I grabbed my bag and headed for the back door. After toeing into a pair of flip-flops, I darted into the garage, wheeled out my bike, stuffed my bag in the basket, and cycled down the driveway.

I biked with abandon, the moonlight guiding my path. I knew my way to Rueland Town Park, day or night, so I could've pedaled there blindfolded.

By the time I cycled over one of the footbridges and arrived at the softly lit gazebo, my pulse was pummeling in my chest and my legs begged for a break. Listening to my sore muscles, I hopped off the bike, leaned it on its kickstand, and flopped down on a nearby bench. With nothing to do but enjoy the moment, I turned my gaze to the flowers and lights twinkling in the gazebo. *Ahhh*. Peace and solitude.

Two cops on bikes rode by, giving a friendly wave. I nodded back, contentment warming me throughout. The truth was, no matter what had happened in the park, it would continue to be the heart and soul of Rueland.

Feeling more myself, I pushed off from the bench and wandered up the shelter's steps, charmed by its everlasting beauty.

I heard a lively Latin tune I recognized from last weekend and spotted a couple hip-hopping down the path. A beat later, another couple strolled by with a Scottish terrier in a plaid vest I'd seen for sale at the Scottish booth. The dog gave a short bark, announcing its presence...or alerting the couple of mine. Cute thing, but it didn't have the personality Mrs. Lombardi's Chester had. Lucky thing.

I gazed along another path leading from the gazebo and saw in the distance another figure approaching, wearing what looked like traditional garb. Sweet. And yet another reminder of the impact from the multicultural fair. Seemed people wanted to keep the event alive in the face of what had taken place a mere week ago.

Curious who the oncoming person was, I leaned on the gazebo's railing and waited to get a better look. From afar, I thought it was a woman. But the swagger was all wrong for a female.

A sudden thought hit me. *Oh Lord*. What if it was Jock, wanting to collect on those ballet lessons? He knew Romero was out of town. *Gulp*. An instant picture came to mind of Jock standing in my living room with only a towel around his toned waist. Sort of like the skirt the approaching person was wearing and why I thought it was a woman.

No. I cleared my head. Couldn't be Jock. I would've heard his bike pull up. People, for Pete's sake, living in

Albuquerque would've heard Jock's bike pull up. *Not true*, a little voice said. *This is a huge park. He could've left his bike anywhere. He could've walked.* But how did he know I was here? Right. Dumb question. The only thing about me Jock didn't know was my bra size. And I had a hunch I was wrong about that, too.

Okay, I had to pull myself together. If it was Jock, I'd deal with it. This was a big old park. Room enough for lots of people to stroll. One thing he could bet on: I wouldn't be giving him ballet lessons in the gazebo at ten o'clock at night. No matter how persuasive he was.

I blinked wide-eyed as the dim light outlined the form, bringing it into focus. I zipped to the steps of the gazebo, my heart hammering a thousand beats a minute. As the figure neared, I could tell he didn't have the wall of chest Jock had or the extreme height. He did, however, have a confident stride, a gorgeous physique, and an eternal five o'clock shadow. Plus, a sexy name and husky voice.

Romero stopped at the foot of the gazebo and locked eyes on me, his hot presence stirring me to the core. His dark hair fell over his fitted jacket, a bowtie adorned his neck, and a traditional plaid kilt hugged his waist. I couldn't remember ever seeing Romero look this handsome and entirely mouth-watering. And in a skirt, no less. A perfect Ken doll with enough scruff to be G.I. Joe. Every last thought vanished from my mind as I gazed hungrily at him.

"Come down here." Sex appeal dripped from his gruff tone, his eyes darkening to *dangerous and ready*.

I swallowed dryly and fought to remain steady on my feet because in another second I was going to melt to the ground. He knew I didn't take orders kindly, but not only was Romero virile and in control, he was also impossible to resist.

Tugging my sweatshirt another inch off my shoulders from his scorching gaze, I climbed down the stairs one at a time. I moved in slow motion, aware his eyes were further stripping my clothes off my frame. Stopping on the last step, aching from being so near, I peered up into his irresistible face, yearning for his strong hands to touch me. "I thought you were in Baton Rouge."

"Wrapped things up early," he said, his mouth breathtakingly close. "Had a bonnie lass to see back home."

I bit hard on my lip, his put-on Scottish accent and deep voice, almost my undoing. It took everything inside not to jump into his arms.

Attempting to act cool and calm, I inhaled the night air that blended with his enticing scent. "How did you know I was here?"

"Where else would I find the most impulsive, intuitive woman I've ever met...especially a week after a murder case in her favorite park?"

My tone softened. "You knew this was my favorite park?"

"From the first moment you discovered MacDunnell." His stunning gaze held mine, his sapphire eyes reflecting the gazebo's lights behind me. "Your determination to see things restored spoke volumes about your love for this place."

There was no fooling Romero. He wore the badge, after all.

"Speaking of MacDunnell..." He opened his pouch hanging strategically in front of his kilt, brought out a small black box, and held it out to me. "Saw this in Louisiana. Thought you might like it."

"What is it?" I was on my tiptoes, trying to keep the excitement out of my voice.

"Open it and find out."

I took hold of the box and flipped up the lid. Sitting on a pretty velvet bed was the most beautiful ring I'd ever seen, a glowing purple stone surrounded by an antique gold scalloped setting. "A mood ring?"

"You seemed mesmerized by MacDunnell's. Thought you might like one of your own." He grinned. "May even help me keep track of your moods."

Not sure if I should be flattered or insulted, I placed the ring on my finger and waited anxiously for it to turn color. "Are you saying I'm moody?"

He chuckled. "Moody, no. Impulsive. Overactive. Excitable. *Yes*. I may be doing myself a disservice since I do enjoy figuring out what your impetuousness will get you into next. But for the sake of interest, why don't we give it a go."

I wanted to point out that *overactive* and *excitable* also equaled *unbalanced* and *high-strung*, but his sweet gesture warmed my heart. And since a mood ring's meanings had played a part in solving the mystery, I was willing to overlook the cost of words this one time.

I thanked him, then looked longingly down the length of his outfit.

"And this?" Apart from Jock, I'd never seen clothes hug a man like they did Romero. I took my finger and followed the pleats down the front of his kilt. "Why are you dressed like a Highlander?"

He laced his fingers through mine and stroked his thumb over my knuckles. "Fair is fair." His gaze fell to my bare shoulders, his sensual aura coming at me like a freight train.

"Sorry?" At this point, I was amazed I was still standing.

He bent his head and seductively placed a small kiss on my left shoulder. "Since your ethnic gear got wrecked, I figured I'd wear mine. I *am* half Scottish, don't forget."

A grin crept up my face all the while I prayed my legs wouldn't give out. "I do like a man in plaid. And I especially like your cute, furry bag." I slipped my hand out of his warm grasp and flicked the tassels on his pouch.

His eyebrows hiked up. "That's a sporran, not a furry bag. And I think my testosterone level just dropped."

That was impossible. Romero was as macho as they came. Big. Strong. Tough. Sexy. He bent to kiss my other shoulder, and I just about climaxed on the spot.

Staring into my eyes, he hauled me closer and slid his hands inside the waistband of my yoga pants. His touch said he'd had enough flirting; his stare said he wanted more.

"A lot of talk last weekend…" His breathing slowed and his stubble scratched my cheek. "People wondering if it's true what they say about men in kilts."

Tingles charged through my body, and my groin throbbed from his touch. I held myself together, not giving any indication I'd had the same thoughts. Sure, they'd been directed at Jock, but that was neither here nor there.

I backed up and batted my eyelashes. "Well? Is it true what they say?"

He put my hand to his mouth, grazed it across his parted lips, then assessed the purple stone on my ring turning to yellow. Giving me an amused grin, he nodded toward home. "You're about to find out."

Making things worse: the dead nun's secret that haunts Valentine, another murder, car chases, death threats, mysterious clues, an interfering mother, and a crazy staff.

Between brushing off Jock's advances and splitting hairs with handsome Detective Romero, Valentine struggles to comb through the crime, utilizing her tools of the trade in some outrageous situations. Question is, will she succeed?

BOOK 3

MURDER, CURLERS, AND CRUISES

In her third fast-paced mystery, beautician Valentine Beaumont and her madcap crew sail the high seas on a Caribbean "Beauty Cruise." When a bizarre murder takes place onboard, Valentine finds herself swept into the middle of the investigation.

If things aren't bad enough, her mother is playing matchmaker, a loved one is kidnapped, drug smuggling is afoot, a hair contest proves disastrous, and a strange alliance between tough Detective Romero and sexy stylist Jock de Marco rubs Valentine the wrong way.

Will this impulsive beauty sleuth comb through the catastrophes and untangle the mystery, or will this voyage turn into another fatal Titanic? With Jock and Romero onboard, it's destined to be a hot cruise!

BOOK 4

MURDER, CURLERS, AND KEGS

In her first action-packed mini mystery, beautician Valentine Beaumont is stalked by an escaped felon she once helped put behind bars. As she strives to stay one step ahead and stop this maniac before he kills her, she stumbles onto a dead body, unearths secret plots, struggles with family obligations, and is tackled in more ways than one.

With a string of beauty disasters, two sexy heroes, a ticking clock, and a little help from her friends, can Valentine solve this case before the killer gets his revenge, or will this be her last?

Murder, Curlers & Kegs is book 4 in the Murder, Curlers series and the first in Valentine's shorter-length mini mysteries.

What's Next in
The Valentine Beaumont Mysteries

MURDER, CURLERS, AND KITES
A Valentine Beaumont Mini Mystery

Book Club Discussion Questions

Enjoy the banter while you share these questions with your book club!

1. Does your city or town hold a yearly event like a multicultural festival?
2. There are many types of ethnic foods served at the multicultural fair in the story. Is there a certain country whose cuisine you love to eat?
3. The park is a safe haven for Valentine. Are there any places that hold a special meaning for you?
4. Is there anything you do to honor your heritage, such as cook traditional dishes, wear customary clothes, listen to cultural music?
5. Valentine's friend Twix explains what the colors on a mood ring represent. Do you think that these rings can predict your moods?
6. Valentine buys a wooden elephant from the India tent at the fair. If you were to visit an event like this, would souvenirs interest you?
7. Romero has done a fair bit of traveling for work. In this story, he was in Louisiana on a case. What is the farthest you've ever traveled for work?
8. The globe mascot was part of the multicultural festival. Do you have a favorite mascot? If so, does it revolve around a town event? A sports team? A Disney character?
9. In this story, Kashi has added a world collection to his brooches. Pick a country and make up a brooch design. What would you name your "Get Out of Town" brooch?
10. Did you have any idea who the murderer was?

Note to Readers

Thank you for taking the time to read MURDER, CURLERS, AND KILTS. If you enjoyed Valentine's story, please consider telling your friends or posting a short review. Word of mouth is an author's best friend and much appreciated. Thank you!

Social Media Links

Website: www.arlenemcfarlane.com

Newsletter Sign-up:
www.arlenemcfarlane.com/signup/signup5.html

Facebook: facebook.com/ArleneMcFarlaneAuthor/

Facebook Readers' Group:
www.facebook.com/groups/1253793228097364/

Twitter: @mcfa_arlene

Pinterest: pinterest.com/amcfarlane0990

Arlene McFarlane is the *USA Today* bestselling author of the *Murder, Curlers* series. Previously an aesthetician, hairstylist, and owner of a full-service salon, Arlene now writes full-time. She's also an accomplished pianist and makeover artist. When time allows, she plays publicly and posts makeovers on her website.

Arlene is a member of Romance Writers of America®, Sisters in Crime, Toronto Romance Writers, SOWG, and the Golden Network. She's won and placed in over 30 contests, including twice in the Golden Heart®, twice in the Daphne du Maurier, and also in the prestigious Chanticleer International Mystery & Mayhem Book Awards.

Arlene lives with her family in Canada.

www.arlenemcfarlane.com

CPSIA information can be obtained
at www.ICGtesting.com
Printed in the USA
LVHW092135241121
704415LV00013B/80